Lady Jane

Lady Jane

EVERY ERA HAS ITS FALLEN WOMEN

BY

Vicki Hopkins

Copyright © 2019 Vicki Hopkins

ISBN: 978-1-7333695-1-0

Library of Congress Control Number: 2019910980

All rights reserved. No part of this book may be reproduced or transmitted in any form or by any means, electronic or mechanical, including photocopying, recording, or by any information storage and retrieval system, without permission in writing from the copyright owner.

This is a work of fiction. Names, characters, places, and incidents either are product of the author's imagination or are used fictitiously, and any resemblance to any actual persons, living or dead, events, or locales is entirely coincidental.

Published by
Red Brick Media
Hillsboro, OR

Dedication

To Susannah Holland, my scandalous second great-aunt, who had a child out of wedlock in 1882 at the age of twenty-two with John William Thompson. He married her eleven years later.

Born August 1, 1860
Blackburn, Lancashire, England
Died April 20, 1931
Moss Side, Lancashire, England

CHAPTER 1
ꙮ How to Break a Heart ꙮ

Jane Cavanagh could not believe she was witnessing a grown man cry. Not just any man, mind you. This was Viscount Berkshire, and it mesmerized her to watch his illogical sobs. His tears dripped on his satin brocade waistcoat. The meticulously stitched garment, fashioned by the best tailor in London, soaked up each droplet as if it were shielding his broken heart.

The dramatic scene added to Jane's long list of conquests and subsequent discards of male companions. Whenever she spoke those fateful words, "It's time for us to go our separate ways," it elicited a myriad of reactions. Men yelled in anger, pleaded with her as if she had sentenced them to death, or were effectively rendered speechless from shock. Nevertheless, this scene—oh, this was an achievement. A grown man, weeping like a baby.

"It's astonishing that you can shed so many tears in such a short period, Neville," she cajoled him, giving him a comforting pat on the arm. "Do you always cry so earnestly over such trivial matters?"

"Triv-trivial?" he blubbered between his wet lips. "You think that breaking my heart is trivial?" His red eyes widened in bewilderment.

"Well, I suppose in the grand scheme of things, perhaps not. I have always admired you as a man of integrity and strength." She stifled a giggle, bringing her hand to her mouth. "Obviously, by your sniveling display, I was terribly wrong."

After taking his handkerchief and blowing his nose, which Jane found rather repulsive over how loud it sounded, he grabbed her hand and began to bargain.

"Oh Jane. My dearest Jane."

"Yes, Neville," she replied, arching a brow in anticipation of multiple entreaties, none of which would move her cold heart.

"What can I do to change your mind? Is it something about me you do not like? I can change, I assure you." He gasped between words. "I'll do anything, my darling, anything to keep us together."

Jane hated to see him reduced to begging, but in desperation, men were prone to theatrics.

"I like you just as you are, Neville. You need not change anything except to stop crying. It's unbecoming, dearest."

Suddenly the viscount dropped to one knee. "I beg you to marry me, Jane. I'm in love with you, and I shall die if you refuse."

Jane exhaled a weary sigh at the pathetic sight. "Viscount, please don't bend your knee. I'm afraid that it shall not alter my decision." She took his hand and attempted to pull him to his feet.

"Why, Jane? You know I'm fiercely in love with you, and I thought you were with me." The viscount stood and crushed her hand in his, refusing to let go. She looked at him with indifference. It did not matter how hard Jane tried to stir up emotion, absolutely nothing rose to the surface. When it came to matters of love, her heart remained unmoved. The same dead, empty void in the center of her soul persisted.

"If I've told you once, I've told you a thousand times, love has nothing to do with it," she reminded him in an unsympathetic tone. "Frankly, I don't believe in the emotion. It's a waste of energy and time."

His brow furrowed at her, and his eyes grew dark. Jane recognized the clear indication that his emotions were now tumbling over into anger.

"I don't understand you," he spouted like a boiling teakettle. "I assumed you loved me." He swiftly dropped her hand.

"Did I say I loved you?" Jane asked with a sour expression. "Well, did I?"

Neville paused, clenching his jaw, knowing she had not once uttered the phrase.

"Well, not in so many words, but you must admit we made passionate love," he insisted. "You acted as if you loved me when we were intimate."

"Yes, I will admit that our romps in bed were very entertaining. You are in my top five of ardent lovemakers, Neville. You should be proud of your artful skills."

"Top five?" He balked as if she had flung the worst possible insult of his life. His mouth gaped open in disbelief.

"Hmmm," she said, bringing her index finger to her mouth and tapping it while pondering. "As I recollect the others again and reassess my tallies, I think that I can safely say you are number three." She shook her head positively. "Yes, number three."

Neville threw his hands in the air and paced back and forth in front of Jane like an agitated primate. She sensed a twinge of empathy for the man, so she attempted to cajole him further.

"Dearest, we had a good eight months together," she began. "Eight months is the longest I have been with any man in years. You should be proud that you now hold the longevity record of my affairs."

Rather than taking it as a compliment, he turned beet red in the face. Perhaps he was going to regress into another crying jag, or maybe he was going to have a heart attack and die at her feet. It would be most inconvenient as she had a social function to attend to in the next hour.

"How could I have been so blind?" he wailed. "You know, other men warned me about you," he growled, shaking his finger in her face.

"They did? How delightful." Jane grinned without an ounce of mercy.

"I should have listened to them. Instead, I threw all caution to the wind, hoping I would be the one man that you would settle with and wed."

Jane pulled her mouth to one side after hearing the terrible idea. "I'm not the marrying type," she emphatically declared. "Besides, I told you this at the start, but you chose not to listen."

"Do you mean to tell me that you have absolutely no affection for me whatsoever and that I have merely been a sexual diversion these past eight months?"

"And a very good sexual diversion, I must say." Jane stepped forward and patted him on the cheek.

He grabbed her wrist. "Don't patronize me, Jane, or you'll be sorry."

Jane rolled her eyes at his next desperate bid for her affections. From tears to bargaining, to pleading, to anger, and now threats. Neville had run the entire gamut of emotions in a matter of minutes. Indeed, he had broken another record.

"I am never sorry for anything that I do," Jane clarified with certainty in her voice. "And I doubt I shall be in the future." She lifted her chin in arrogant defiance. "We had a good go of it, Neville, and I enjoyed myself with you. Nevertheless, I'm bored, and it's time to move on."

"Bored?" he spat out. "How can you be bored?

I don't understand you, woman," he croaked with emotion.

"Dearest, your heart will mend. I am sure a fine woman is waiting for you somewhere in London who will snatch you up next season. The ton is full of desperate young ladies seeking titled aristocrats. Unfortunately, the fact of the matter is I'm not one of them."

Jane walked toward the door of Neville's sitting room and glanced at him before departing.

"I hope when our paths cross again in the future that we can be friends." She warmly smiled. "You would be surprised how many men call me such regardless of our previous relationship and ultimate separation."

Neville shook his head negatively. "I shall not call you one, Jane. I'd rather ruin you like you've ruined me and God know how many others."

He walked toward her and stood tall, pulling his broad shoulders back. She had to admit that she would miss his handsome face. Tall men had a way of making her weak in the knees, except for today. When she first met Neville, he had swept her off her feet quickly with his smooth talk and exciting personality. He had just inherited his title at the passing of his elderly father. Well respected among his peers, he had a gregarious personality she enjoyed. Moreover, he took care of her needs in bed most pleasantly.

Like with her other arrangements, his

feelings for her deepened. Jane found herself withdrawing. Once a man showed romantic attachment, she severed the relationship and moved on.

"Spitefulness doesn't suit you, Neville," she said, sad that he displayed so much animosity over the matter.

"One day someone will break your heart, and I hope I'm there to see it." He curled his lips into a wicked grin. "And by God, I'll have a good laugh when they do."

"That's a cruel thing to say to a lady," Jane complained, scowling at him. "Perhaps it is a good thing that I take my leave now."

"You, madam, are no lady!" He hurled his final insult. "You are undoubtedly the most ruthless woman in London."

A deep sigh expelled from Jane's lungs as she gazed at Neville. It was shameful to witness the viscount lower himself to such degrading tactics. Nevertheless, the fact remained. His words carried no threat from the brokenhearted man whose eyes remained bloodshot because he cried like a baby.

"I bid you farewell, Neville." With those words, Jane crossed the threshold but heard Neville curse under his breath. She thought he said "Witch," but perhaps he said "Bitch." No matter. Many men had called her a variety of scornful names in the past. With her unfeeling heart, they bounced off and fell at her feet, powerless to hurt her in return.

It took seconds to forget about Neville as she climbed into her waiting carriage and told the driver to take her to the Whitmore residence. By the end of the week, she would be out hunting again before the season ended. A duke might be a nice feather in her hat for an affair. It would probably garner a few comments in the gossip column. Regardless, she had no desire to be a duchess as they merely bore heirs and oversaw the workings of the household. Marriage would never be on the table, but entertainment always remained welcome. Any aristocrat would do if it cured her boredom and they bedded her well.

As the carriage traversed the city streets, Jane loosened the drawstring on her embroidered reticule and pulled out a small piece of parchment. She opened the folded note and familiarized herself with the names jotted down by Lady Whitmore, her aunt. It contained a list of social events throughout the city as the season neared its conclusion.

In the next hour, she would be with a group of ladies to hear the latest gossip regarding eligible men. If you wanted to know who was who, this was the place to have tea in the afternoon—behind the closed parlor door of Lady Whitmore.

Chapter 2
The Gossip Mill

Not a gossip column in all London compared to the private meetings that four ladies held on a weekly cadence. Millicent Whitmore was the queen of wagging tongues, and she was also Jane's aunt. In her company came three other fine ladies of title—Phoebe Westlake, Claudia Lindsley, and Daniella Boggs. All the ladies had married aristocrats, but they came from long, distinguished bloodlines themselves. What did they have in common? A throng of female and male children all in need of spouses. Each season they came together to plot how they could conveniently match their offspring who had come of age with the perfect mate to blend family fortunes.

Jane, on the other hand, had arrived as a guest in need of introductions and invitations to the few remaining social events of the season. After all, she had been out of circulation for eight long months. Now that the viscount had been put aside, Jane could focus upon her next conquest. Of course, he had to be a mature male, an avid lovemaker, distinguished, titled, outrageously handsome, and easily manipulated. Every woman needed a man who would cater to her whims, and Jane was no different.

The carriage slowed and halted at her aunt's town house, and Jane shoved the note back in her reticule. A quick pull of the drawstring closed it tight. Her driver opened the door, and she gave instructions.

"I'll be about two hours or so. You can either wait or return to fetch me later," Jane advised.

"As you wish, my lady," he replied, closing the coach door behind her as she stepped onto the pavement.

Jane approached the door and gave the knocker a hearty rap. It soon opened, revealing Mr. O'Flaherty, the butler at her aunt's seasonal town house.

"Ah, Lady Jane," he said, opening wide the door. "All the ladies are in the parlor at present. Your aunt awaits your arrival."

"Thank you," she replied, sauntering down the hall. The closed door indicated the juicy discussions had already started. Jane gave it a quick knock, turned the handle, and poked her head around the doorframe.

"It's just me," she announced with a silly grin.

"Oh, darling Jane." Her aunt Millicent greeted her. "Come in, dearest."

Jane entered, closed the door, and smiled at the ladies gathered together like a circle of cackling hens. An empty space on the settee next to Lady Westlake remained, so Jane settled down and made herself comfortable.

"Tea, dear?" Her aunt poured a cup, added a pinch of milk, and handed her the rose-pattern china.

"Yes, thank you. I'm parched," Jane admitted, taking a quick sip.

"You know everyone here, I believe," Millicent commented.

"Yes, but I don't think I've had a formal introduction to Lady Boggs," Jane admitted.

"Well, you need no introduction, young lady," Lady Boggs responded. She eyed Jane with curiosity, taking particular care to admire her dress. "Your reputation is well spoken of, Lady Jane."

"You are too kind," Jane admitted, grinning. "It is often ill spoken of, I'm afraid."

"How did it go?" Millicent reached over, touching Jane's arm with a concerned glint in her eyes.

It proved impossible to stifle a laugh, and Jane giggled, recalling the viscount's tears. "He cried," she chortled. "Cried like a baby."

"Who cried?" Phoebe asked, eyes widening and leaning forward for the first tidbit of juicy gossip.

"Viscount Berkshire," Jane chuckled. "It's the first time I have witnessed a grown man weep."

"Am I to assume that you've cast off the poor

viscount?" Daniella inquired. Her brow furrowed. "Our family is well acquainted with him. Such a kind and generous man."

"Oh, I do not disagree with you," Jane clarified. "I had no complaints regarding his companionship whatsoever. However, I never commit to long-term relationships as I tend to become bored."

"Easily bored," Millicent replied cynically.

"Well, I for one am terribly envious of you," Claudia said. "You are absolutely stunning in appearance, free to do as you will, and have men begging for your companionship."

"You're too generous as well," Jane said, beginning to feel a bit puffed up from the accolades.

"Youth—how I miss it." Claudia sighed with a wistful stare in her eyes. "When I married my handsome Gregory, I never imagined that twenty-five years later I'd be trying to marry off eight children."

"Didn't we all," replied Phoebe, her countenance souring. "We are terribly envious of you, Jane."

Perhaps they should be jealous. Thankfully, Jane had an ample allowance from her tolerant father, who accepted her lifestyle with little complaint. It had given her the autonomy to do as she pleased without the need to be a kept woman. Jane enjoyed male companionship more than being with a group of women and loved to prance around society wrapped in the arm of a handsome man. A good acquaintance kept her entertained with social activities, spirited conversation, and above all, passionate encounters in bed.

Although each relationship Jane experienced had been pleasurable, she never understood the gnawing emptiness that plagued her soul. She enjoyed her freedom and lack of sensual restraint, which gave her a scandalous reputation in society. By all accounts, Jane should be the happiest woman in London. As she gazed at the ladies who hung upon her every word, she realized they misguidedly envied her freedom. To put it in perspective, she spoke the truth.

"You are correct in your assumption that I am free, but freedom sometimes does have a price." Her confession fell on deaf ears as the next question clearly rose from the gutter.

"You must tell us, Jane, how did the viscount perform behind closed doors? I'm dying to know," Claudia poked with an irreverent smirk on her face.

"Ladies," Jane laughed, watching them lean in her direction. They looked like hungry dogs, waiting for a treat to be tossed.

"Do tell us," Millicent prodded.

Surprised that even her aunt wanted to hear the delectable gossip, she relented. "Well, if you insist." Jane took a sip of her tea first and then continued. "I told Neville that he ranked number three out of ten conquests, but apparently, I wounded his ego by not placing him as number one."

"Heavens! Have you really been intimate with ten men?" Claudia asked, wide-eyed.

Before Jane could answer, Phoebe interjected.

"Who is number one?"

Hearing the mention of number one incited Jane's aunt to interject herself into the conversation. With her brow knitted, she advised the women in a stern tone, "We don't speak of number one . . . ever."

Jane's glittering eyes dulled, and she lowered her head to gaze into her nearly empty teacup. The very mention of number one resurrected a tight sensation in her chest as if she were suffocating. It always did, and she hated it. Jane quickly steered the conversation elsewhere.

"Well, now," she said, clearing her throat of the lump that had formed. "What is the latest news of the season? Who is engaged and who remains available?"

The ladies glanced amongst themselves and back at Jane's aunt who tilted her head, indicating the topic should change. A silent understanding passed between all in the room. Some matters, even among close acquaintances, should not be spoken about, especially when it concerned a lady's heart.

Millicent looked at Claudia. "Well, I know

you are anxious to make an announcement, Claudia. Tell us the news."

She brought her hands together and clapped them in a gleeful move. "My daughter, Bernice, received a proposal from Edmund Duvane."

Thank goodness Jane had not been sipping tea, or she would have choked. Edmund, that rascal, had finally found a match. She could not help but wonder if Bernice's daughter had been privy to his roguish dalliances before bending his knee.

"The firstborn of the duke?" Phoebe inquired, wide-eyed.

"Yes, that's the one." Claudia closed her eyes and sighed in relief. "My daughter will be a duchess one day."

Jane's brow arched. "A happy duchess, I hope." As soon as the words left her mouth, she regretted the comment. Claudia shot her an alarming glance as if she had doused her delight with a bucket of cold water.

"Whatever do you mean?" she inquired.

Jane remained silent. She glanced at her aunt, hoping she would save her from the awkward moment. Instead, Millicent shot her a disapproving glare in return. It only took a few more moments of Claudia pondering before the answer became clear.

"Jane Cavanagh, don't tell me that you have been intimately acquainted with the man?" Her eyes narrowed at Jane, demanding the truth.

Jane inhaled a breath and tried to remain nonchalant. It was not her style to express remorse or act uncomfortable about her past relationships. Nevertheless, she sat among her aunt's dear friends and did not wish to cause an uproar or hurt anyone's feelings.

"Well, not *that* intimate," Jane replied with an innocent glance. "I merely had a few dinner engagements with the man, but it went no further." It was a bald-faced lie but a necessary one to keep the peace. "I'm sure she will be delighted with Lord Duvane, and your daughter will make a wonderful duchess one day." She smiled demurely, keeping up the charade. "Congratulations on your success!"

Of course, her involvement with him reached far beyond a few dinners, but that was over three years ago. She had long forgotten him once she found out he was a rogue at heart. Why that bothered her, Jane had no idea. After all, she was as wicked to the core as any scoundrel in London with her recurring relationships.

"Why do I get the feeling that many of the prospective husbands for our girls may have crossed your path in the previous years?" Daniella asked, pulling her mouth to one side. The other ladies chuckled over the prospect as well.

"Look at it this way, ladies. If they have, I have merely left a wake of broken hearts for your beautiful young daughters to pick up and comfort. They will all be safer in their arms rather than mine."

"Well put," Millicent remarked. "You break them, and young ladies will mend them."

Jane smiled shyly as if she were an innocent angel. After taking a sip of tea, it was time to get down to business.

"So, what functions might I engage myself in these coming months before the season ends? I'm anxious to dip my toes back in the water."

Her aunt's guests glanced at one another, a bit wary at her question.

Chapter 3
∽ Unsettling News ∽

The next few hours were thoroughly enjoyed by Jane as she sat and listened to the ladies tell their tales of success or failure in matching their offspring. A few of the names mentioned were unknown, but Jane, of course, had not bedded every man in London. By the end of the session, she had garnered invitations to a ball at Lady Westlake's residence and an upcoming soiree at Lady Boggs's. Satisfied that a few openings were available, Jane readied herself to bid farewell to her aunt.

"Stay for a few more minutes," Millicent entreated. "We need to talk."

With a serious look on her face, Millicent closed the parlor door and pointed to an empty chair. "Have a seat, dear," she insisted with a stern voice.

A bit taken back by the solemnity of her request, Jane obliged. "Is everything all right, Aunt? You looked terribly concerned about something."

"Would you like a drink, Jane?"

"No, thank you. I have had enough tea to last until dinnertime."

"No, I mean a real drink. I have some excellent raspberry brandy you might enjoy," she said, nodding at a crystal decanter on the sideboard.

When Millicent mentioned alcohol before a conversation, it usually meant an unpleasant topic would soon begin.

"I'll pass on the brandy," Jane said. Unable to understand the change in Millicent's demeanor, Jane took a wild guess behind its meaning. "Is Father asking you to give me a lecture?"

"No, no, nothing of the sort," Millicent replied, dismissing the question. "My brother has no qualms regarding your choices in life. Nor do I, for that matter. But . . . "

"But what?" Jane encouraged her with an anxious tone. "What is it you wish to say?"

"Well," she began, inhaling a breath, "last Friday eve, I attended a private dinner party at Lord Postlethwaite's residence."

"Postlethwaite," Jane chuckled. "I'm always mispronouncing that man's name."

"Yes, quite a mouthful, I agree," Millicent noted. "Are you sure you don't want a sip of brandy?"

"Auntie, out with it, please. I don't want brandy," she balked in agitation. "What are you trying to tell me?"

It took a few moments for Millicent to speak.

She inhaled and exhaled. Opened her mouth and then shut it again. With a ragged breath, she finally spoke. "There was a surprise guest in attendance."

Frustrated at the mystery, Jane blurted, "What guest?"

"Oh dear, I can hardly speak the man's name," Millicent groaned. "Perhaps, I'll just say . . . number one."

Number one.

As soon as Jane heard those two words, the blood drained from her face. A moment later, she surely appeared like an ashen marble statue. Unable to move or breathe, she brought her hand to her throat as if she were choking for air.

"Oh my," Millicent said, rising to her feet and heading for the sideboard. She poured a spot of brandy into a crystal glass and hastily brought it back to Jane, placing it in her hand. "Drink dear, before you faint."

Jane's trembling hand brought the liquid to her lips, and she gulped the brandy in a matter of seconds. When she closed her eyes, the room spun around in circles. On the verge of collapsing, she determined to pull her senses together before making a fool of herself over the announcement.

"Do you need another, Jane?" Millicent asked softly.

"Another what?" she said, glancing up at her aunt hovering above her body.

"Drink, dear."

"No, no, I'm fine," she said, handing the empty glass back to Millicent. After taking a few moments to compose herself, she asked a question. "How—how long has he been back?"

"Two months, so I'm told."

Two months. Jane could not believe that he had returned to England. She had known the day would come but never anticipated that it would affect her to such a degree. Inside her chest, Jane sensed her heart flutter, skipping beats now and then.

"And how—how is Matthew?" she asked, her voice trembling.

"He's Colonel Rutland now, dear, a decorated war hero, wealthy, and very much respected by his peers."

A colonel. His goal achieved.

"His father, Sir Charles, must be very proud. I remembered when he purchased his commission. Matthew was ecstatic." Jane lowered her eyes, trying not to conjure up too many memories of the past. "Well, it's good to hear that he has done well for himself." Jane's emotions bubbled up, threatening tears, but she kept them suppressed. Acting as if the news had no further consequence, she asked the inevitable. "Is he married with children now?"

Millicent hesitated for a few moments, causing Jane to wonder about the pained expression on her face.

"What is it, Auntie?"

"I'm afraid that his wife passed away last year, poor soul, giving birth to their first child, who was stillborn."

"How dreadful," she mumbled. Upon hearing the sad outcome, Jane's coherent thoughts vanished. It had been too much to process in one sitting—Matthew's return, the death of his wife, the possibility their paths might cross.

Jane rose to her feet, grabbed the empty glass Millicent held in her hand, and headed to the decanter. After pouring an ample amount of brandy, she took a large drink to dull the shock of his return. As memories flooded back, she shook her head, hoping to send them flying elsewhere.

Millicent came to her side and put her arms around her waist, giving Jane a hug. "I'm sorry, dear. I know how upsetting this must be for you."

"A shock and a surprise, yes, but I shall not confess that it upsets me," Jane lied. "The past is the past. He chose his career path, married, went to war, and now he's back." She nodded as if to agree with her assessment. "It's been nearly nine years. I shall not allow it to deter me in my quest for another lover, nor shall I weep over lost loves of the past, if you get my meaning." Jane emptied the glass and set it down, thankful for the alcohol that flowed through her veins, bringing a sense of relief to her nerves.

"Shall you be attending the ball and soiree that your friends are holding?" Jane inquired, wanting to change the subject.

"Oh, I wouldn't miss it for the world. I may not have sons or daughters any longer to marry off, but I cannot miss another social gathering during the season. You know how I love to watch the interactions and gossip about it afterward." Millicent animated her excitement with a little clap.

"It's why I love you so much," Jane said, giving her an embrace in return. "Now, I must be off. My poor driver must be getting antsy waiting for me outdoors." Jane gathered her shawl and handbag and smiled warmly at Millicent. "I shall see you soon."

"Will you be purchasing a few new dresses for the occasions?" her aunt asked with interest.

"You know, that's an excellent idea," Jane said. "Since I'm on the prowl again for companionship, a new frock may do just the trick." Anything would do the trick if it kept her from thinking of him. Shopping had always been a cure for overthinking.

After a goodbye peck on the cheek, Jane left and climbed into the carriage, giving orders for her return to her modest town house only a few blocks away. Her father rented a small residence in London for her use, as she no longer wished to live at their family estate. As a young woman of twenty-eight, Jane had grown far beyond the need for a chaperone. Instead, she had chosen her own path in life rather than relinquishing to the expectations of society and duty. Like a spoiled child, Jane had become used to her overindulgence for pleasures in life.

She was a lady of her own making—independent, outgoing in personality, and uninhibited when it came to sexual exploits outside marriage. Jane flitted from man to man, being a mistress to no one. The practice of receiving money or gifts for her companionship was not her style. Because of her self-sufficient status, she had no need to be beholden to any man. In doing so, she had gained a controversial reputation. Those who disapproved avoided her in social circles, but plenty of men and women found her fascinating.

Despite her lack of morals, she was meticulously careful not to get pregnant by insisting on English riding coats or men spilling their seed elsewhere. Over time, Jane became proficient at giving men pleasure outside of her body, if they reciprocated the favor. She also recognized the rhythm of her menses, abstaining during certain times of the month. After all her precautions, she realized that each time she enjoyed intimacy, she played a game of roulette, and accidents could happen. So far, she had been fortunate.

Only one incident in her life had molded the woman that she had become, and only one man she held responsible for the outcome—Matthew Rutland. He had ruined her physically and mentally at the tender age of eighteen. As a result, her heart had grown cold and her character wild and uninhibited because she failed to resolve the consequences of unrequited love. Jane concluded that if men could wantonly use women without scruples, then she, too, could do the same.

When the viscount wished for her to suffer a broken heart, little did he know that Jane had already grieved the devastating effects the experience produced. As far as she was concerned, women agonized far more than men did when it came to such matters. In fact, Jane convinced herself that men did not love—they only took what they needed when it came to the female sex. Nevertheless, she had to admit that Neville had come close to convincing her that the male species might be able to feel the emotion, albeit for a short time. She had yet to meet a man devastated beyond measure when it came to loving a woman. Usually, all it took was the next skirt to rise, a quick sexual encounter, and all was right with the world.

As she returned home, her housemaid Betty greeted her at the door. "Is there anything I can get you, your ladyship?"

"No, I'm fine. A bit sleepy though."

Tired from the long and emotional day, Jane walked into her parlor, kicked off her pumps, and reclined on the chaise. The alcohol that she had gulped at her aunt's home flowed through her veins, making her eyes heavy. Naps were not her usual pastime, but it sounded tempting to take one as she leisurely stretched out. She started to slip into a peaceful sleep when a loud banging came at the front door. Startled, she sat up. "Who is that?" she asked.

"A message for you, my lady. Just delivered."

Betty handed Jane the note and left her alone. She glanced at the writing addressed to her on the front of the envelope but did not recognize it. At first, Jane thought the viscount might be making another plea for her to change her mind. She slipped open the seal, pulled out the parchment, and burst out laughing.

"Now that you've rid yourself of boring Neville, will you finally give me the time of day? I am still enamored with you, Jane. Let it be my turn. I promise to keep you laughing the entire time, even between the sheets. Lord Grisham."

"You devil," Jane roared aloud. The man was an utter delight when it came to his humor, though not quite as handsome as she preferred. Bedding him was not a priority, but his sense of comedy might be precisely what she needed. Jane folded the note and placed it back in the envelope. Tomorrow she would write him a wickedly teasing reply. For now, she still needed to retreat to a place where her mind could rest. The last thing she needed to do was think about the return of Matthew Rutland, because it hurt far too much.

CHAPTER 4
∽ The Return ∽

Matthew held the small bouquet and placed it on Felicity's grave, alongside that of his son. He had named the boy Benjamin, after his grandfather, who had been a significant influence in his life. As he stood there, he noted a few weeds creeping up along the marble monument, and he bent over and pulled them out of the hard, dry soil. When he was satisfied with the appearance of the memorial, Matthew stepped back and spoke to his dead wife.

"I cannot believe the anniversary of your death nears." He grimaced as if an old wound had opened in his chest. Matthew stood, thoughtfully gazing at the place where she lay. "My father tells me to move on with my life. What do you think, my love? Can you forgive me if I seek another wife?"

He waited to hear her voice echo through his soul, but the grave remained silent. Felicity had moved on. It was not like the days after her demise when he continued to feel her presence wherever he went. Matthew thought she remained nearby for his sake. As time passed and her spirit diminished, he recognized that she had gone wherever souls depart to. Indeed, hers had gone to heaven, along with their newborn son, who never inhaled a single breath after leaving her womb.

"I suppose that I do need to move on, Felicity," he somberly said. "Why does it hurt so much?" Matthew struggled with a mixture of guilt and expectation while clutching the rim of his hat. Separating loyalty to his wife and anticipation of falling in love again had not been easy. "Perhaps Father is right to encourage me, darling. To be honest, I am lonely."

The love that he once held for Felicity remained carefully tucked inside a corner of his heart, but it no longer burned as adoration does when one is alive to reciprocate the emotion. Grief lingered, nevertheless, over the loss of the son he would never know. Something inside told him they were together and happy. He could live with that knowledge, knowing they were at peace.

After ensuring that the flowers looked presentable, Matthew put his hat back on and strolled back to the manor house. He had recently returned from his last tour of duty a few months ago, entering semiretirement. Napoleon now being in exile had brought relief, and Matthew needed a reprieve from military service. In the interim, he would receive half pay, but he could be called back to active duty if the need arose. He prayed that day would never come.

Admittedly, it was time for him to seek another spouse. The process of searching for a woman who could match Felicity's gentle goodness would be daunting. He held her in such high regard that it was difficult for Matthew to contemplate that another female could ever fill her place.

Last week he had attempted to make an effort to return to society by attending Lord Postlethwaite's dinner party. At his father's prodding, Matthew had accompanied him to the gathering, feeling like a fish out of water. The awkward social interaction reminded him of how used he had become to living with hardened soldiers in uniforms who lacked refined social skills. It would take some time to acclimate himself to the change in scenery. By evening's end, the dinner party had turned into an opportunity to make new acquaintances.

To his surprise, however, he did notice the familiar face of Lady Whitmore, who eyed him curiously. He had not seen the lady for over nine years and tried to remember the circumstances. It took a while before clarity returned and the remembrance of her niece, Jane, came into mind. The resurrection of that part of his life brought uneasiness, so he had quickly dismissed it. The rest of the evening he had avoided a face-to-face conversation with Lady Whitmore and hoped that any future social interactions would be sparse. By now, Jane was undoubtedly married with children of her own. Enough time had passed between the two to bury the unfortunate incident.

The long, leisurely walk back to the estate cleared Matthew's head. His father's ancestral home, Rutland Park, sat thirty miles from the city. A week ago, his father had returned from London, ending his participation in the season early. As a baronet, he rarely felt the need to remain for the entire time. The only reason for attending was to see old friends. Sir Charles preferred the estate to any pleasures or entertainment that London provided. Also, his arthritis had become increasingly painful, making long periods of standing or walking difficult.

Matthew, however, had decided to relocate to their small family town house in London from March to June to attend a few functions rather than traveling back and forth. Now that he had left active duty, he could leisurely enter back into society. It would allow him time to look for a new wife or at least gain companionship to fill the void in his life. He was not getting any younger either, and he desperately wanted children. Sir Charles had taken the loss of his grandson as hard as Matthew, looking for a new male to continue the Rutland ancestral line.

As Matthew approached the front entrance of the manor house, he noted a carriage. He glanced at the crest on the door and smiled, spotting the recognizable family heraldry. An old friend must have heard about his return and had come to pay him a visit. Matthew's step quickened as he came indoors and recognized voices in the sitting room. He rounded the corner and stood in the threshold excited to see a familiar friend, speaking with his father.

"Neville, you rascal," he exclaimed, grinning from ear to ear. "You're a sight for sore eyes. How good it is to see you again." Matthew grabbed his hand and shook it heartily while giving Neville a pat on his upper arm.

"God, it's good to see you!" Neville bellowed. He eyed Matthew up and down as if he were looking for wounds. "Sir Charles, you must be glad that your son is back safe and whole," he commented, glancing over at Matthew's father.

"Indeed, I am." Sir Charles gave an agreeable nod.

"Well, I'm glad to be back as well," Matthew cheerfully responded.

"I'll leave the two of you alone to catch up," his father announced.

"Thank you," Matthew replied. After his father retreated from the room, Matthew smiled broadly, taking in the appearance of his old friend. He looked well. Still the handsome viscount, sporting a thin mustache and a thick head of wavy hair. Neville appeared a bit thinner than the last time Matthew saw him but still in good shape overall.

The two of them had formed an alliance while attending university together and forged a friendship that Matthew believed would last a lifetime. Neville had been a pillar of strength for him when he lost Felicity. When he returned to the front, it put a distance between them that survived with a few letters. It had been nearly a year since they had taken the opportunity to speak face-to-face. Neville's arrival came at a perfect time.

"Drink?" Matthew asked. "Whiskey or brandy, old friend?"

"Three fingers of whiskey, please."

"Three fingers? A bit much, but whatever you need." After pouring a glass for each of them, Matthew handed one to Neville. "Come, sit, and let's talk."

"I read in the paper you returned with medals as a hero, Matthew. I am so thankful you did well. I had to come to see for myself." Neville sat down in a large, overstuffed chair, relaxing and sipping his drink. Matthew sat down across from him with a pleased smile remaining on his lips.

"Yes, I've returned, although I daresay England lost many good young men." Matthew took a large gulp. "Visions of battlefields that I hope to forget."

His smile faded as scenes of the carnage he had witnessed flowed through his mind. Good young men, indeed, cut down in the prime of life. Why he had been spared he would never know. Perhaps Felicity's prayers had kept him safe, added with his father's as well.

"I cannot imagine how difficult it must be, but you were always the one who wanted the military life. Now look at you, a decorated colonel."

Matthew grew tired of the constant recognition of his medals and so-called bravery. Eager to turn the attention elsewhere, he put the focus on Neville instead.

"Enough of me, Neville. What of you these days? How are your estate, sisters, and things in general?" His eyes glanced over his friend's body again. "You look well. I don't see a portly roundness you've always worried about developing in your midsection." Matthew smirked.

"No pudge yet," Neville said, patting his stomach. "Well, Julianne married last season as you know. Her belly is swollen with child, and she is due any time now."

The news naturally raised a note of caution in Matthew's soul. Childbearing was a risky business, and Julianne was a sweet tiny thing.

"My prayers will be with her for a safe delivery and healthy child," he said solemnly.

"And Susan?"

"This is her first season of husband hunting."

"And what of you, dear friend? Any ladies caught your eye yet?" asked Matthew.

Neville's smile disappeared in a flash, and he lowered his gaze to the alcohol in his glass. "I'm afraid not," he replied in a bleak tone.

Shocked by his answer, Matthew's brow knit together in skepticism. "I cannot believe you are still a bachelor, almost thirty, in a season filled with determined debutantes desperate to catch a titled husband." Matthew took a sip of his drink and studied the strange reaction of his friend, who stared at the carpet. A second later, Neville shifted uncomfortably in his chair and then took another sip of whiskey.

"Good Lord, man, why the morose state of mind?" Matthew asked, pressing him for an answer.

"I'm nursing a broken heart at the moment," Neville somberly admitted. "Hence, the three fingers of whiskey in this glass."

The surprising answer brought a surge of empathy for Neville. Matthew understood that broken hearts came in many forms—from the loss of a loved one in death to a loss of a loved one from a broken relationship.

"How disappointing," Matthew said kindly. He paused for a moment, giving Neville a minute to contain his emotions. If he did not know any better, he would swear that his friend's eyes watered from the admission. "Do you want to talk about it?"

"Well, there's nothing much to say except that I fell hard and foolishly for a woman. She sank her claws into my heart and then without forewarning pulled them out, leaving it shredded to pieces." Neville's voice deepened to a tone of bitterness.

"Dear Lord," Matthew sharply replied. "She sounds more like a tigress than a lady by the sound of your voice."

"Tigress," Neville mused. "I'm afraid that I have other names for her that are less gentlemanly in nature." He gulped the remainder of his drink.

"I'm sorry to hear of it," Matthew responded, thinking of some words of wisdom. "I suppose love is like learning to ride a horse. Sometimes you fall off, but you get back on."

"Oh, I fell, all right," Neville agreed with a modest grin of amusement. "Next time I'm going to seek a bit of pleasure instead of looking for love and a comforting woman. I'm not too keen to get back on the proverbial horse so soon unless it's a pleasant ride."

"Ah, I see your off-color humor remains," Matthew said with a lopsided smile. He sat for a moment, pondering. "God, a comforting woman," he mused aloud. "It's been so long that I fear I have forgotten what it's like." He finished the alcohol in his glass as well and thought of getting another. He held his glass up. "Would you like a refill?"

"Please," Neville said, handing his over.

As Matthew rose to his feet and walked to the

decanter, Neville asked a nagging question.

"Tell me, Matthew. Are you ready to seek a wife again?"

Matthew poured the drinks, pondering how to answer the question. Upon returning, he gave one to Neville and sat down. Only a half hour ago, he had admitted to Felicity that he was ready to move on. Loneliness gnawed at his soul, and he wanted—no he needed a companion. He was not the type of man who enjoyed being alone. Now that his military career was on hold, he could search for a mate.

"I believe that I am, although I'm not sure I remember how to go about the process of seeking one." Matthew swished the alcohol around in his glass, deliberating the problematic task. "All the social interaction and the ins and outs of courtship are enough to make a man dizzy."

"Perhaps to begin with you should seek a little pleasure," Neville suggested with a sly grin. "I know a few ladies who might give you a bit of comfort before you start the hunt."

Matthew arched a brow at Neville's suggestion. He had not been the type of man to seek out morally loose women for a momentary release. Perhaps Neville was right though. An uncomplicated but satisfying night here and there might do him good. God knew he needed an enjoyable romp with the opposite sex. It had been far too long.

"I'll keep that thought in mind," he replied.

"I'm assuming you have recommendations where I might find such encounters."

"Yes, but I've been out of the loop, so to speak, these last eight months thanks to my recent heartbreak." Neville heaved a deep sigh. "Damn, that woman was a hellion under the sheets," he unashamedly admitted. "Not an ounce of inhibition."

"You mean you bed her unwed, and she was willing?" Matthew could not comprehend that Neville had courted such a woman. By the sorrowful look in his eye, it appeared that he loved her deeply.

"She has a bit of a reputation," Neville admitted. "Foolishly, I believed I would be the one to capture her affections and make her my wife."

"Interesting," Matthew mused aloud. "If that's her nature, however, I doubt anyone will cage the tigress in the future."

"I doubt it as well. She uses men and discards them. Apparently, I became a bore, and she's moving on to her next conquest."

"Well, then good riddance, I say," Matthew replied. "You probably should be thankful you've been spared further damage."

They both fell into silence, each pondering the recent conversation. Matthew could not help but wonder who the woman was who broke his friend's heart. It was a good thing that he had not divulged her identity, or Matthew might give her a piece of his mind for how she treated Neville if they ever met.

"I'll be in London in a few days," Matthew announced.

"Where are you staying?"

"At our small town house, but this is the last season. Father intends to sell afterward as he rarely spends time there any longer. In fact, all the staff has been dismissed except one lonely housemaid who occasionally comes to clean."

"I'm in the city at our residence but come and go," Neville said. "We should attend a few social functions together. Two handsome bachelors seeking women. We'll have the season leftovers desperate for husbands clamoring for us both."

"Clamoring," Matthew bellowed a hearty laugh. "I suddenly have this vision of being mobbed by undesirable, desperate spinsters."

"Oh, good God," Neville groaned. "If it comes to that, I'll certainly introduce you to a few other beautiful creatures with no morals." After downing the last drop of whiskey, he rose to his feet. "I must be off."

Matthew stood and patted Neville on the shoulder, flashing a friendly smile of goodwill. "Good of you come. I desperately need a diversion, and it appears you are the man to take me down that road."

After saying a final goodbye, Matthew watched Neville's carriage leave the estate. His visit had been timely, and a sense of adventure filled Matthew's soul. Perhaps the next few months would provide him with entertainment and good company.

Chapter 5

Opened Wounds

The ball held by Earl Westlake and his lovely wife had been widely anticipated. In attendance would be Aunt Millicent and the other ladies of the gossip circle. Lady Westlake's second daughter, Penelope, still sought an acceptable suitor, and Lady Boggs was optimistic for her youngest daughter, Rose.

Jane held some concern that she may run into Bernice Lindsley and her new fiancé, Lord Duvane. The interaction might prove awkward, but for Bernice's sake, she should feign any knowledge of his lordship to keep everyone from conjecture or embarrassment. The prospective bride need not know Jane had joined her body with his occasionally, rating him a mere eight in her ten-best-lover list. She hoped he had improved somewhat, or Bernice may never find satisfaction in the marriage bed.

As she entered the ballroom, her eyes widened at the grandeur of the setting. The walls of gilded plasterwork were decorated with large floor-to-ceiling mirrors that caught the light of the many candelabras throughout the room. A massive crystal chandelier hung in the center, lit with hundreds of candles. When she lifted her eyes, a beautiful fresco ceiling with cherubs looked down on the attendees. A small orchestra sat upon a raised platform at the far end. Bouquets of roses sat on stands throughout the room. Earl Westlake certainly spared no expense at his residence nor lacked generosity when it came to entertaining guests. No doubt a sublime menu of delicacies would be served for supper.

Even though she had arrived early, the room was crowded with guests milling about. The musicians sat tuning their instruments, getting ready to play the first selection. The earl and Lady Westlake greeted everyone's arrival, and Jane expressed her thankfulness for the invitation.

"Thank you so much for inviting me," she said.

"You are most welcome," Lady Westlake remarked. "This is Millicent's niece, Jane," she announced to her husband.

"Lady Jane, welcome," the earl said, giving a quick bow.

"How beautiful everything appears, Lady Westlake," Jane remarked favorably.

After Lady Westland took account of Jane's appearance, she expressed concern. "You are so pretty, Jane, I fear that every gentleman's eye shall be yours this evening. My poor Penelope shall be overshadowed by your presence."

Lady Westlake eyed her gold-colored evening gown of silk embroidered with flowers at the neckline, sleeves, and hemline with black and gold threading. Long ivory gloves covered her hands and arms, and Jane had chosen a necklace of perfect white pearls with a pendant. Two ostrich feathers adorned her headdress, and she clutched a fan in her hand.

"My dear Lady Westlake," she assured in a kind tone. "My interest this evening will only be in men who are far older than the young gents who will court your beautiful daughter." She leaned in and whispered in her ear. "I need an experienced, older man," she smirked, drawing back. Jane glanced around the room and took an assessment of the crowd. "I daresay there appear to be many young gentlemen available for Penelope to meet."

Jane gave another courteous nod of her head and then glided into the throng of attendees. It did not take long for her to spot her aunt a few feet away, chatting with Lady Boggs. Anxious to insert herself into the conversation, Jane approached, but not before plucking a flute of champagne off a tray held by a footman.

"Good evening, ladies," she said, eyeing their outfits as well. Millicent looked quite ravishing for her age, flouting more feathers in her hair than Jane. Even Lady Boggs stood out as a picture of middle-aged beauty.

"Are you discussing anything of interest?" she asked. At that moment, the small orchestra began their first piece, drawing multiple men and women to the central focal point of the ballroom for the first dance.

"Jane, you look delectable," her aunt remarked.

"I've been told," she smirked in return. "Anything worthy of note this evening?" Her eyes scanned the perimeter.

"My daughter, Rose, is already dancing," Lady Boggs announced. "It appears Lord Grisham's son, Percy, has taken a shining to her."

"Grisham?" Jane repeated. Her eyes cast another quick glance around the room, wondering if he was about to corner her at any moment.

"Don't tell me Lord Grisham has . . . ," Millicent began, but her words trailed off.

"Oh no, not Grisham. He's not my flavor of tea, if you catch my drift, although he wishes to sweeten my cup."

Millicent laughed aloud, and Lady Boggs's eyes grew wide. As she continued to glance around the room, to her horror, she spotted Neville in the far corner. He was talking with another gentleman, whose appearance she could not view because he faced in the opposite direction.

"I see Viscount Berkshire is in attendance," she noted. "Apparently, his heart has healed, and he's on the hunt."

"Where?" Millicent said, peering around.

"I should go speak with him and ask how he is getting on," Jane remarked, stepping away.

"Jane," Millicent called frantically after her as she made her way across the ballroom. The music, dancing, and copious amounts of loud conversation had drowned out Millicent's panicked voice.

Jane witnessed Neville catch her approach, and his face turned ashen. Swiftly, he averted his gaze, and he said something to the gentleman standing across from him. Regardless of the outcome of their last meeting, she did hope that they could remain friends. Perhaps this would test his willingness to agree to the new arrangement. Jane arrived within a few feet of where he stood and smiled at Neville, who acted oblivious to her presence.

"Hello, Neville." She greeted him in a warm and friendly tone. "How are you?" At last his eyes shifted in her direction with a distinct shade of bitterness remaining.

"I'm doing well, thank you," he replied coldly. The gentleman nearby did not move, which she found slightly odd. Neville must have realized his rudeness in not making an introduction and suddenly spoke. "May I introduce you to Colonel Rutland," he announced. "He is a good friend of mine."

Jane was not sure exactly what happened after those words were spoken, except in the next second, the glass that she held in her hand fell to the tiled floor. When it hit, liquid and shards of crystal splattered at her feet. When Matthew turned around and looked at her, the room spun in circles, but she maintained her balance despite it. She saw his face, but nothing registered with clarity. Perhaps her soul had stepped out of her body. At that moment, she distinctly felt as if a knife had reopened the wound in her heart. Unable to speak or move, she stood there with splashes of champagne dripping down her skirt.

"Good God, Jane!" Neville bellowed as liquid speckled his trousers and shoes. His loud voice pulled her from the stupor that had enveloped her, and she brought both hands to her mouth, gasping. "Oh, I'm so sorry, Neville," she said. "It just slipped from my fingers." Thankfully, a footman witnessed the incident and hastily came over to assist in cleaning up the mess. He kindly suggested that they move a few feet away while he attended to the spill. They did and came together in a circle of three and halted.

"I've never known you to be clumsy," Neville said, brushing his wet pant leg a few times. Matthew had apparently avoided the brunt of the spray.

"No doubt I'm the cause," Matthew sullenly remarked. "I'm acquainted with Lady Jane, but it's been some years since we've seen one another."

"Acquainted?" Neville barked loudly, causing

a few heads to turn in their direction.

"Indeed," Jane replied. "Perhaps it was the shock that caused my hand to lose its grip."

Neville's eyes widened in what Jane could only term as sheer horror. The ashen countenance he had a few seconds ago had suddenly turned into a blush. To make matters worse, Jane sensed the blood rush to her own cheeks, which probably burst as red as the roses on the nearby table.

"You mean to tell me the two of you know each other?" Neville babbled out of breath.

"Well, it was a long time ago," Jane said, dismissing his concern. "How long has it been, Matthew? Eight, nine years since we last exchanged words?" She hesitated and narrowed her eyes at him, her astonishment morphing into loathing.

Matthew's lips pressed in a hard line, obviously understanding the drift of her comment about their last words exchanged. The ghost of their past resurrected in her memories, haunting Jane as she stood, waiting for him to speak. At that moment, she distinctly recalled his departure and the ensuing devastation.

"Yes, nine years, if my recollection is correct." Matthew turned toward Neville and spoke in a low tone. "Is she the acquaintance you spoke about?"

Shaking his head in agreement, Neville verbalized what Matthew wanted to know. "Yes, this is Lady Jane, who cruelly dispensed of my services a few weeks ago."

"I dispensed of your services?" Jane replied with an arched brow. "Perhaps we should clarify that I had been the one dispensing services." She unashamedly glanced at Matthew. "The fact of the matter is, Colonel Rutland, your friend here is responsible for the disruption of our relationship."

"Bollocks," Neville loudly swore, gaining the attention of everyone within a five-foot perimeter.

Jane snorted a giggle, knowing that she had riled him. Obviously, the man was not about to remain friends.

"Well, regardless of who dispensed with whom," Matthew stated, "it appears emotions between the two of you are still raw."

Jane shifted her gaze back to Matthew. It hurt to look at him because he had matured into an extremely handsome man. Being in the military had molded Matthew into a formidable specimen who exuded sexual attraction like none other in the ballroom. He was taller than she remembered, and oh, how she liked men who towered above her. Perhaps she enjoyed the dominance when men had their way with her, making her weak and helpless when she wielded power in the bedchamber.

Whatever the reason, between his height, broad shoulders, a full head of brown hair, and blue eyes that could melt the winter's snow, she knew old emotions would soon resurrect to cause havoc. As her gaze crawled lazily up and down his form, her body wanted to ravish him. If it were not for the fact that she hated him to the core, it would have made for a delightful evening.

"Well, then I shall be gracious and retreat back to my aunt on the other side of the room. No doubt you two gentlemen will be looking for young ladies to dance with this evening, and I would not wish to be an obstacle in your pursuits."

"And what about you?" Neville snidely inquired as she turned to walk away. Jane halted and glanced back over her shoulder at him. "Are you out and about, looking for your next victim?" he snidely prodded.

"You exaggerate, Viscount Berkshire. I never make men victims, only companions." She nodded her head at Matthew. "Colonel Rutland, it's been a pleasure to see you again."

With those words, she intentionally put one foot forward in front of the other to put distance between her and the gentlemen. She had not expected to run into Matthew and certainly had not been ready to face him after all these years.

By the time she returned to Millicent's side, her aunt had detected her distraught countenance and trembling hands.

"I tried to call after you, Jane, when I realized he stood by the viscount, but you didn't hear me."

"Sadly, I did not."

"How was it, dear?"

"Painful. More than I imagined," Jane replied with a quivering voice.

"Whatever do you mean?" Lady Boggs asked.

"Number one, Daniella," Millicent replied, narrowing her eyes. "Let it go."

"Oh, I see," Lady Boggs replied solemnly. "Oh, look. Here comes Lord Grisham."

Jane lifted her eyes and saw him prancing in her direction like a deer in rut. With his balding head and pudgy stomach, he looked directly at her with a broad smile across his face. She inhaled a deep breath, knowing the man wanted a dance.

"Ladies, how are you this fine evening?" he said, bowing at the waist. He reached out his hand toward Jane. "I've come to ask Lady Jane if she would do me the honor of this next dance."

Jane needed a diversion, and if his humor could pull her out of the shock, Grisham was the man to do it.

"I would be delighted," she said, taking his hand. A moment later, they were dancing the quadrille, and Jane's heart grew lighter. If her peripheral vision kept away from where Neville and Matthew stood, she would survive the remainder of the evening.

Chapter 6
ᑲ The Wretched Past ᑲ

Matthew watched as Jane left his company, astonished at their meeting after all these years. More surprising was the fact that his friend had been with her for the past eight months in an intimate relationship. He could barely accept as truth that she had become such an untamed creature. By now, she should have settled down, been married, and borne a handful of children. Instead, she had lain claim to the most notorious reputation in London society. It left him thunderstruck.

"My damn trousers are still wet," Neville complained. "Can you believe she dropped the flute of champagne?" He glanced over at the footman, who finished wiping the wet floor and scooping up the broken pieces of glass.

"I cannot grasp that it is Jane Cavanagh," Matthew said in a ragged breath. His gaze followed her in astonishment as she sauntered across the room. Jane's steps were gracefully assured and her figure faultless. The dress clung to her body in perfect symmetry as the silken fabric shimmered down her frame with each step. She carried an aura of a goddess about her, and people noticed her as she passed them by—especially the men. Suddenly, Neville snapped his fingers in front of his face.

"Stop gawking at her," he ordered. "You're making a scene."

Matthew shook his head to bring back a sense of reality and sheepishly glanced at Neville. "Sorry. I'm just shocked at the sight of her and more shocked that the two of you . . . " He could not say the word.

"Copulated?" Neville snickered in a low tone. "Yes, we did, and often. The woman is wild in bed. If you need a good romp without any attachment, she's your lady."

Matthew's head turned, looking for her again, and he noted she no longer stood with her aunt. Instead, he noticed her in the middle of the dance floor. His eyes continued to follow her movements, mesmerized by her presence.

"Who is that man she is with?" he asked, nodding in her direction.

Neville glanced and then burst out laughing. "Good God, it's Lord Grisham. He's wanted to slip up her skirt for as long as I can remember."

"He doesn't look her type," Matthew flatly remarked. Oddly, it bothered him, watching their interaction on the dance floor.

Once again Neville snapped his fingers, and Matthew frowned at him, annoyed by his action.

"All right, all right. I'll stop staring," he said. "I just can't get over it."

The footman walked by with a tray of champagne, and Neville grabbed two glasses. He shoved one in Matthew's direction. "Here, drink this. You look like you need it."

Without complaint, he brought the spirits to his lips and took a sip. He did need a drink. In fact, he needed more than a drink. Matthew could not reconcile what had happened to Jane. It did not make any sense. Not only had her personality changed into an unrecognizable creature, but her physical characteristics had sucked the breath from his lungs. He remembered that she was a pleasant-looking girl at eighteen, but now she had turned into a deity of rare beauty. Her flawless skin, dark eyes, hair, and curves were enough to send any man to a happy and satisfying death. If those attributes were not enough, her lips were plump and her breasts rounded. Good God, the woman had changed, leaving him captivated.

"So exactly how well did you know Jane eight or nine years ago?" Neville asked, finally gaining his attention.

With great difficulty, Matthew turned and pulled his eyes away. Neville wanted answers, and perhaps deserved them, but Matthew choked from the thickness in the air. Either that or guilt had returned to strangle him underneath his tight cravat.

Matthew noticed two double doors in the middle of the room that were open. It appeared they led to an outdoor veranda. Out of breath, he suggested they take the discussion elsewhere.

"Why don't we have a private word, and I'll tell you," he proposed. "Let's step outside." After gulping the remainder of his champagne, he set the flute down on a table. A moment later, the fresh air greeted his nostrils, and he inhaled a deep breath. He glanced around the exterior location, which was a small garden with stone walls. A couple spoke quietly off to the left, and Matthew headed right to the far border of the enclosure. Neville followed. When they were out of hearing, he stopped.

"I should have grabbed another champagne," he said, eyeing Neville's remaining drink.

"Here, take the rest of it," Neville offered. He shoved the glass in his direction, and Matthew took it without hesitation.

"Thanks." After taking a sip, he appreciated his friend's patience, because it was going to take a few seconds to gather the courage to tell him the story. Of course, it was not a story which would imply that he had made the entire fiasco up in his mind. No, it was the truth—the painful, ugly truth.

"You remember how impetuous we were during university?" he asked.

"Sure, we had our share of drink and women along with the studies. What of it?"

Matthew sighed. "When I returned home, and before my father purchased my commission, I met Jane at a local assembly dance. We found each other's company agreeable, and I began to court her with the serious intent of marriage."

"Good Lord, Matthew. I had no idea." Neville leaned against the wall. He crossed his arms in front of him and listened intently.

"Well, I'll get right to the point," he sharply admitted. "I took her virtue."

"Bloody hell, you devil," Neville croaked. "Took it or did she give it?"

"Well, she gave it willingly. I did not force myself upon her if that's what you're considering," Matthew's voice grated with a tone of irritation.

"Did you love her?"

Matthew frowned and shrugged his shoulders. It was difficult to recall precisely what emotions he experienced nine years ago. He did not remember any kind of love compared to that which he held for Felicity.

"When I recall, I don't think I did. It wasn't until Felicity came into my life that I truly loved any woman." He gulped the remainder of the alcohol and let out a sigh afterward. "I thought we would make a good match, and my father had suggested it was time for me to marry. Even her father approved of the marriage."

"Then why didn't you?"

The question tore at his soul, and Matthew

ran his fingers through his hair. Agitated that he had to resurrect the past, he grimaced as he admitted what occurred. "Jane got pregnant from our joining. Naturally, I did the proper thing and asked her to marry me, but before we wed, she miscarried." He blurted it out in one quick sentence, hoping that it would not sear his conscience again.

"Good God, man. I'm at a loss for words," Neville said with a gaping mouth. He stared at Matthew wide-eyed for a few moments, attempting to make sense of it.

"Afterward, I begged Father to purchase me a commission. He liked Jane and found my decision to be a disappointment but had not been aware of the pregnancy. Eventually, he agreed."

"What in God's name did you tell Jane?"

"Well, I don't remember the exact words, except that I wanted to call off the engagement because I was leaving for the military."

Neville stared at Matthew for some time as he stood rigid, holding the now-empty glass in his hand. Matthew worried that he might be on the verge of losing a friend over the incident and had no idea what Neville thought of him now. The stern look upon Neville's face slowly faded, and his eyes lit up.

"Makes sense now," Neville said, shaking his head affirmatively. A crooked grin upturned the corner of his lips.

"What does?" Matthew shot a quizzical

glance, not understanding his statement.

"Why she uses men, that's what. You broke her heart, and she's never recovered," he said with firm assurance.

Immediately reasoning it absurd, Matthew dismissed his assumption. "Oh, I don't believe that for one bit. It was a long time ago. Surely whatever feelings the woman held for me are long gone and forgotten."

"Oh, I agree, they are long gone, but it's left her with bitterness that she carries to this day." Neville smiled wickedly. "She may taste as sweet as nectar in bed, but when she's done with a man, she casts him aside without a second thought as she perceives you did to her."

"I didn't cast," Matthew balked. "I told her I wasn't ready to marry."

"Were those the last words exchanged between the two of you that she referred to a few minutes ago?"

Matthew lowered his eyes. As he recalled the moment, he had to agree, it was not a pleasant one.

"She took it rather badly. That I will admit." His lips twisted as he remembered. "Many tears were shed. She pleaded one moment, became angry the next."

"Sounds vaguely familiar," Neville admitted. "And you held no remorse?"

"Of course, I felt remorse. I did not mean to hurt Jane, but I also wanted a career in the military more than anything. I knew it to be my calling, and I didn't think one foolish error of my youth should prevent me from pursuing my goals." He lowered his eyes, feeling justified and embarrassed at the same moment. "The fact of the matter is, I made a mistake, and I assumed she would meet another man and marry. By now, after nine years, all should have healed and been forgotten."

Matthew sensed that Neville was studying him or perhaps even judging him about the past. He hoped it would not put a strain upon their relationship. After all, he had just relieved his soul of a dark secret that he kept locked away for years. Their friendship meant a lot to him, but then he realized he probably offended him for not sharing the incident before now.

"I apologize, Neville, for not telling you sooner," he confessed in a contrite voice. "I consider you a close friend, and for the life of me, I'm not sure why I never spoke of it." He paused, analyzing his actions. "Perhaps, I feared you would think less of me. I'm not sure," he admitted, shaking his head.

"Don't worry about it," Neville replied. He reached out and patted Matthew on the shoulder. "It is not as if I wrote to you these past eight months either, confessing my out-of-wedlock sexual tryst with Jane." He chuckled and lowered his eyes to the grass underneath his feet. "I daresay, Matthew, I feel most peculiar that we have both shared the same woman."

"As do I," Matthew admitted with a sly grin. He glanced back toward the door and saw couples dancing. Jane flitted by, apparently with another gentleman. Once again, it bothered him, and he did not know why. A sense of protectiveness rose in his gut, which made no logic whatsoever. He frowned and then pulled his eyes away from the door.

"You know," Neville began, "You are probably both very different people now. The years have changed you."

"No doubt," Matthew agreed.

"Do you wish to find out how much?"

"What?" Matthew frowned at his suggestion.

"You heard me. I have a feeling that the two of you have unfinished business."

"Now it is my turn to say bollocks," Matthew retorted, glowering at him over the ill-advised remark.

"Well, if you are looking for an easy encounter, she's your lady." Neville snickered.

Naturally, he admitted bedding a beauty such as her would be a welcome bit of comfort—but this was Jane, for goodness' sake.

"There's no way in hell I'm going to bed that woman," Matthew scoffed. "Are you out of your mind?" He could not believe Neville proposed such a thing. Perhaps the consumption of too much alcohol had incited his ridiculous suggestion.

Neville leaned away from the wall and stood in front of him. "Let's put it this way. There are a few months left in the season. You are in London. She is in London. The two of you are going to cross paths again at other social activities—it is a given. The question remains—what are you going to do about it?"

"Well, I'm doing nothing about it, especially if you still hold lingering feelings for her. It wouldn't be right."

Neville waved him off. "Don't worry about me. I'm sure I'll get over it." He took a step back toward the ballroom. "I'm off for another drink. You coming?" he asked, pushing past Matthew.

He headed for the door, leaving Matthew behind to stew about their conversation. Seeing Jane had resurfaced a forgotten portion of his life he had shoved into a dark closet of his past.

"Bloody hell," he cursed, heading back indoors, in need of alcohol. All he cared to do for the rest of the evening was to avoid Jane at all costs.

CHAPTER 7
~ Midnight Supper ~

Although Jane immersed herself in the entertainment of the evening, inwardly the scar over her wounded heart slowly opened. With each step of the quadrille and feigned laughter at Lord Grisham's jokes, she could swear that she was bleeding internally and would soon fall dead at his feet. How could one man have such a profound effect upon her soul when in the past nine years she had failed to feel anything for another human being? It defied all reason, angering her that she lacked control over her emotions.

Jane easily played the coquettish flirt with various dance partners, building around herself a shield of protection. Despite her efforts, the troubling fact remained that Matthew occupied the same room as she did. Earlier she had caught sight of him disappearing out the double doors with Neville. No doubt the viscount had shared with him everything, causing her even more distress as the evening wore on.

Eventually, Matthew and Neville both found dance partners, partaking in the festivities.

Between sets, Jane wandered over to her aunt, seeking refuge. Millicent was fully aware of Jane's past involvement with Matthew and had been with her through the heartbreak. Jane's mother had passed away when she was only five years of age. Being the only child, her aunt had taken the place of mothering her as best as she could. Throughout the ordeal, she never shamed her over the matter but supported her even to this day. Jane knew that her aunt understood her choices after Matthew departed and the motives that drove her existence.

"What do you say?" Lord Grisham inquired, catching her alone again after she had danced with him at least three times.

"About what, your lordship?" She batted her eyelashes at him, teasing the poor soul.

"About you and me, of course." He flashed a wicked grin and winked at her.

Exhaling a weary sigh, she patted him on the arm, trying to let him down gently. "I'm taking a break, your lordship, and resting. The viscount wore me out, and I need to regain my senses before starting another relationship." She cajoled him further with a lie. "I'm not saying no, Lord Grisham. Just not now."

The sparkle in his eyes dulled, and he shook his head. "Of course. I understand, Jane." He appeared to accept his fate. "Alas, I am heartbroken but shall respect your decision." He gave her a curt bow.

Grateful that he was chivalrous enough to walk away and be a gentleman about it, Jane glanced around the ballroom. At the present time, she didn't want to approach any other man at the assembly. She eyed a few, danced with five or six, but no one caught her interest. The only thing that repeatedly held her attention was the whereabouts of Matthew, making matters far worse.

As the hour neared midnight, the attendees became restless, and supper was announced. Jane walked alongside her aunt into the grand dining room. Some guests had left the ball earlier, but at least fifty or more people remained to partake in the lavish spread of food. Neville and Matthew attached themselves and sat purposely at the opposite end of the table. Lady Lindsley's daughter Bernice and her fiancé, Lord Duvane, sat a few seats away from Jane. She luckily had avoided the man throughout the evening, and he dared not give her a second glance.

As expected, the Westlakes had spared no expense as far as the menu. They opted for a hot supper of roasted chicken, beef, and veal, supplemented with vegetables, cheese, bread, and boiled eggs. The many footmen waiting on guests poured the wine, making attendees even more gregarious and drunk while filing their stomachs. The evening ahead would continue to three or four in the morning, and with all the emotional turmoil and the copious amount of spirits she'd consumed, Jane felt exhausted.

She entered small talk with her aunt and those nearby, occasionally glancing at Matthew. It appeared Neville had attached himself to a young lady by the name of Charity Atwood, who acted as if she hung upon his every word. Matthew occasionally conversed with others. Intermittently, he would catch her eye, and she would swiftly avert her gaze in another direction, cursing herself for even looking at him.

Then to her dismay, Lord Westlake spoke loud enough to gain everyone's attention.

"I would like to make a toast to a distinguished guest at our table," he announced. "Colonel Rutland has returned, a decorated war hero, having participated in the defeat of Napoleon." Everyone lifted their glasses, the men rising to their feet, while the ladies remained seated. Jane did as well.

"Thank you, sir, for your service, and welcome home, Colonel Rutland."

"Hear, hear," the men replied.

By the mortified look on Matthew's face, the earl's kind gesture had apparently embarrassed him. He nodded and thanked everyone, then quickly returned to his meal, saying something to Neville. Jane remembered how he never liked to be the center of attention. With his heroism and service, that character trait obviously remained.

It was peculiar to recall the appeal he held for her nine years ago. Jane pondered how much he had changed. No doubt he noticed her transformation too. Neville had probably painted her character as a wicked woman, breaking the hearts of men everywhere in London. She smirked as she pondered making him her next victim in a bid for revenge. Perhaps she should wield her charm until he fell in love with her and then turn around and discard him as he did her years ago. It would be sweet vengeance, and she wondered if it would bring her satisfaction.

Then she suddenly remembered that Matthew already suffered, having lost his wife and son. She frowned. Fate had brutally broken his heart. In fact, he had lost two children, and she wondered if he carried an ounce of grief about their lost child. Jane chastised herself for not saying something earlier to express her condolences. Instead, she had reacted to protect herself, taking control of the situation to her advantage. At moments like this, she really did believe she no longer possessed a heart.

"What are you pondering about?" Millicent asked. "By your furrowed brow, it can only be one thing."

Jane shook her head. "Oh, I'm sorry," she sighed. "You're right, I am thinking about far too many things that I should not be."

"Well, I do applaud how you have maintained your composure this evening."

"Do you?" Jane asked, looking at her directly. "It's been a dreadful act on my part," she admitted with a shaky voice. "I'm afraid seeing the colonel has stirred far too many memories."

"Well, if you're overwhelmed, my dear, why don't you slip away after supper? No need to stay the entire affair unless you have some reason. Perhaps a good night's sleep will help clear your mind."

Jane glanced at Matthew again. He was talking to Neville and laughing about something. Whatever it was, he did not appear to have suffered an ounce of pain after seeing her again. The familiar sense of loathing returned.

"I shall take your advice, Auntie, and leave within the half hour."

As soon as supper ended and guests milled about for a few more dances before the event's end, Jane bid good night to her aunt. After thanking the Westlakes for an enjoyable evening and feigning a headache to justify her early departure, she headed for the door. Her driver had arrived and waited for her down the street.

After retrieving her shawl and handbag, she approached the door, and a footman held it open. Jane was about to step outdoors when a voice called from behind. Instantly, she recognized Matthew's tenor tone.

"Jane, are you leaving?"

Slowly, she turned around and faced him. He stood a few feet away with a furrowed brow as if he felt concerned by her early withdrawal. She, on the hand, began to tremble at the sight of him.

"Yes. I have a slight headache and am tired," she replied.

"I'm sorry to hear of it."

He took another step closer, and Jane's body stiffened at his nearness. She did not wish to be in such proximity to his person. Obviously, he wanted to say something else, but she did not want to hear it. Rather than prolonging the moment, she turned to step outdoors.

"It was good to see you again," Matthew finally admitted. "Perhaps we will cross paths again before the season ends."

As her heart pounded in her chest, and an actual headache began to develop in the back of her skull. She could only muster a glib reply.

"Perhaps we will." With those words, she stepped down the stoop and onto the sidewalk. She had not the heart to turn around and look at Matthew. The universe had asked too much of her this evening, and she possessed nothing more to give.

It was disheartening to see Jane leave as he had hoped to have a few more words with her after supper. Her short reply and lack of enthusiasm to speak before departing indicated she did not want to put the past behind them. Neville was correct—there remained unfinished business between the two of them. In the past nine years, he had not given her a glancing thought. After all, his life had been filled with marriage, grief, and war—not a good combination of life events.

Troubled, he meandered back into the dispersing guests. Neville approached and pointedly asked. "Did she speak with you?"

Matthew shook his head negatively. "She had no interest in doing so. Merely bid me good night and disappeared outdoors."

"Shame," Neville remarked. "I will admit that she was not herself tonight."

Matthew arched a brow. "Jane certainly didn't act that way. Obviously, she's quite proficient in flirting with men."

"True, but I do know her somewhat, Matthew. It was an act for your sake."

Agitated, he frowned. "I must be tired," he admitted, "because my encounter with her is beginning to weigh on me." As he considered returning home, he saw Lady Whitmore approach. Neville noted it as well and swiftly excused himself.

"I'll give you privacy," he said, stepping away.

"Colonel Rutland," she said. "It's a pleasure to see you again."

"And you, Lady Whitmore." Matthew bowed and attempted a weak smile.

"I couldn't help but notice that you met Jane this evening. Were you surprised?" she asked in a sardonic tone, briskly fanning herself.

"Surprised is not the word that I would use to describe my reaction," he remarked. "Stunned more aptly reflects my initial thoughts."

"Stunned by her beauty or stunned by her reputation?" she pressed with a cold look in her eye.

"Naturally both," he replied with an even tone. He realized that Lady Whitmore did not intend to carry on a polite conversation and wished to provoke him for some odd reason.

"Well, you can thank yourself for her reputation, Colonel," she mockingly replied, twisting her lips at him in displeasure.

"You are the second individual this evening to suggest that I hold some responsibility for her choices in life." She had attempted to slice him with her words, but he would have none of it. "How she chooses to live is her decision, Lady Whitmore."

"Perhaps you are correct, Colonel. Nevertheless, the choices we often make are motivated by the events in our lives that have formed us in the crucible, if you will."

Matthew discarded her innuendos. Yes, perhaps Jane had suffered when he chose the military over her, but he had subsequently suffered through the fires of hell himself. Annoyed by the conversation, he decided to end it instead of giving her aunt the satisfaction of confessing any responsibility concerning Jane's character.

"If you will excuse me, Lady Whitmore, the

evening has proved tiring as well as this conversation."

Matthew retreated and found Neville. "I'm going home," he said. "You coming?" The tense tone in his voice revealed his frustration.

"An unpleasant conversation, I surmise," Neville noted, watching Lady Whitmore walk away in a huff.

"I'd rather not talk about it," Matthew spat out. "I'm going home."

As a friend, Neville knew to leave well enough alone, and they both departed after expressing their thankfulness to their hosts for the evening. As they climbed into the carriage, Matthew struggled with the gnawing reality that he had damaged Jane's heart upon their parting. Regardless, time should have healed the wounds. It was beyond his comprehension why she had not married and settled down with another man. The workings of a woman's heart were too complicated to contemplate or make sense of when it came to female emotions. He had learned that much in the few years of his marriage.

Too weary of think further, he pulled his thoughts to Felicity. Speaking with her, even in his muddled mind, often brought a semblance of peace. Tonight, he needed to confess to her departed soul the matter involving Jane. He had kept that secret hidden. No doubt Felicity watched him from heaven, knowing the sordid details already. Perhaps the dead looked down to watch humanity play out their deeds. He hoped she would grant forgiveness for his youthful folly and give him some sense of wisdom on how to handle Jane going forward.

Chapter 8
～ Unfinished Business ～

Sleep eluded Jane for hours after her return home. Now reaching the noon hour, she decided to rise from bed and get a bite to eat. The evening before had been an utter catastrophe. In fact, Matthew's return to society ruined everything. How was she supposed to find another man to entertain her with the past tagging along behind at every turn? No doubt he would be at functions, and their paths would cross again. The entire scenario was infuriating.

A small part of her almost regretted letting Neville go. It was terrible timing, indeed. Things would be much simpler had they still been sharing each other's bed when Matthew arrived. It was uncanny that Neville never knew about her relationship with Matthew, or at least she assumed that was the case. Maybe she should invite Neville back into her life out of spite, considering it would be a wicked thing to do. Revenge appeared to be controlling her thoughts rather than good sense.

Jane headed downstairs, clad in her blue silk

robe. She loved the sense of silk next to her naked skin. It gave her a sense of entitlement and sensuality that no other fabric provided. With her cup filled with hot tea laced with her usual milk and a spot of sugar, she heard her maid answer the door. A moment letter, she came in and handed her a calling card.

"Who in God's name wants to bother me now?" she complained, grabbing it. Viscount Berkshire had decided to drop in uninvited, and Jane knew precisely what the man had come to talk about after last evening. She could quickly turn him away. After all, she was not even dressed yet. As Jane glanced down at her robe draping open to reveal her bare chest, a wicked grin curled her lips, and she decided to tease him for sport.

"Invite him in, Betty," she said, setting his card down on the tabletop. Neville walked through the dining room door and halted when he saw her appearance. Jane could not help but laugh at the look on his face.

"Come in, Neville, and have a seat. You've seen me in less than this robe, so don't let that stop you."

He nervously cleared his throat. "I assumed you would be dressed by now."

"I had a late night," she replied sarcastically, "and felt like sleeping in."

Neville chose a chair across the table from her and with great difficulty kept his eyes focused on her face. She could not help herself and leaned forward, revealing her cleavage. "Would you like a cup of tea?"

"No, I'm fine. I've already drunk too many cups this morning," he said, glancing at the treasure beneath Jane's robe.

"Do you miss it?" she drawled with a mischievous grin.

"You know I do, Jane. Even now, I could rip that damn robe off you, lay you on the tabletop, and have my way with you."

"Then why don't you? I am feeling a tad needful this morning," she moaned. "I didn't realize how difficult it would be to cut off our intimacy in one slash. It has left me aching. Perhaps I should have weaned myself away from your bed instead."

"Close the gap in your robe and stop tormenting me," he hissed. "I didn't come here for you to toy with my heartstrings or receive an invitation to foreplay."

Jane obliged and pulled the separating fabric together. "Then what did you come here for? Another plea for me to take you back?" she asked mockingly.

"I am not so foolish as to believe you would grant that request, especially after last night."

"Oh yes, last night," she coldly remarked. Jane took a sip of tea and avoided looking directly into Neville's eyes. Soon he would begin prodding her for information, poking at her wounds. Regardless, she had her own questions that she wanted to be answered. "Am I to assume that you knew about Matthew and me before we met? If that's not the case, did he enlighten you last evening?"

"Last night was the first time he spoke to me about it," Neville admitted in a low voice. "Frankly, I was astounded at the revelation."

"And how is it that you know the colonel? I'm curious."

"We attended university together and remained friends throughout the years. Albeit, we have not always stayed in touch since neither was aware of our associations with you."

"Interesting," she remarked. "Fate has apparently played a rather interesting joke upon all of us, don't you think?" Neville sat, staring at Jane, and her irritation at his presence rose. "What is it that you want with me, Neville? I have things to do."

"I'll come right to the point and spare you the niceties."

"Do," Jane encouraged him, leaning forward again.

"I told Matthew last eve that I thought the two of you had unfinished business, and I'm inclined—no, obliged—to say the same thing to you." He leaned back in his chair and crossed his arms.

"Whatever business we had concluded nine years ago," Jane flung in return. "He told me his father purchased a commission, and he left. What more do either of us have to say after all this time?" She picked up her teacup and took a sip, watering her dry mouth. When she did, she noticed her hand tremble and damned herself inwardly for her show of lingering emotions.

"You look as if you're about to drop that teacup like you did the crystal flute last night. I suggest you put it down before you do," Neville scolded.

The cup clanked harshly on the saucer, and Jane swore. "Damn it," she grumbled in a deep voice.

"Do you mind me asking you a question?"

"Of course I mind," Jane shot back, still angry that her bodily actions betrayed her emotions.

"Good. I'll ask it then. Do you still love him?"

She rolled her eyes. "Oh, don't be daft, Neville. I told you numerous times that I do not love. It is an emotion I find overtaxing and useless. You, above all people, should realize that by now."

"I'm quite aware of your thoughts on the subject," he replied in a ragged breath. "You might find this hard to believe, Jane, but I had fallen in love with you and really wanted you to be my wife."

"But I told you—"

"Yes, I know what you told me." He cut her words off in frustration. "As I see it, whatever transpired between you and Matthew nine years ago has enslaved you into a belief that all men should be treated in the same manner as he meted out to you."

"And what if I do?" Jane shot him a daring glance. "It serves me well."

"Bollocks."

"What is it with you and that damn curse?" Jane's pent-up emotions caused her to bellow a hearty laugh. At least she didn't break down in tears. "Every time you say that word, my mind wanders to body parts a lady shouldn't contemplate."

"Yes, my favorite term," he chortled. "Would you rather that I say nonsense and make it more ladylike?"

"No, that's quite all right." They fell silent for a moment, and Neville gazed at her with lingering affection. Purposely, she closed her eyes and heart to those amorous gazes he always gave her when he became romantic. Admittedly, she knew that he had fallen in love, and that was why she needed to end the relationship. Sexual intimacy for pleasure gave her freedom. The idea of idealistic love suffocated her. He might as well have put a pillow over her mouth and smothered her to death than speak of marriage and children.

"You should at least make an effort to talk to Matthew if nothing else," Neville suggested.

"There is nothing that I need to say to him. It was all said nine years ago." The idea of rehashing the past in any conversation with Matthew made her nauseated. "I considered making him my next victim," she admitted with a sly grin.

"Oh, I see," Neville remarked in a disgusted tone. "Dangle the bait, catch his heart, reel him in, and then eat him afterward." He negatively shook his head at her unsavory suggestion. "This may surprise you, Jane, but the man has suffered quite a bit in his own life. You're not the only one to have a heart shattered into pieces."

Remorse flood Jane's conscience, and she pulled her eyes away from Neville's harsh glance. It took a moment and a deep breath to admit her insensitivity. "Yes, I heard about his wife and baby," her voice quavered. "It must have been a terrible loss to him personally."

Neville suddenly pushed back his chair and stood up. "Well, I've done what I came to do," he announced. "I've spoken my thoughts to you and Matthew alike after observing your painful reunion, and there it must remain."

Jane rose and walked over to Neville, standing in front of him. He looked rather handsome when he became a tad harsh in his mannerisms. In her bare feet, she stood short and insignificant next to him but noted that he smelled quite good. Neville must have dabbed himself with a new fragrance of cologne.

"You smell good," she remarked, drawing closer to him. "Are you sure you don't want to slip your hand beneath my robe, fondle me, and then throw me on the tabletop?"

He placed both his hands on her shoulders to halt her further encroachment toward his body. "You are incorrigible, Jane."

After giving her a glancing kiss on her cheek, Neville hastily departed, closing the door with a slight bang. The satin belt around her waist loosened and fell to the floor, causing her robe to reveal her nakedness underneath it.

"Damn, you could have done that a minute ago when Neville was in front of me," she complained, snatching it up.

As she returned upstairs to put some clothes on, she grumbled under her breath. "Unfinished business." What did Neville expect her to do about it? As far as she was concerned, nothing needed to be finished between them.

The memory of her pregnancy came flooding back, overcoming her with an emotion that brought tears to her eyes. When Matthew had learned of her condition, he promised to marry her and make things right. After all, she had lain with him and had given him her virginity. Her foolish heart fell irrationally in love with him, so much so that when she lost the baby a week before their wedding day, she wanted to die. If the child had survived, things might have turned out different. He would have married her, and perhaps a fine son or daughter would have come from their union together.

The cold hard truth of the matter had been that he did not love her as she did him. There existed a vast disparity of affection between the two. He held no devotion to her well-being. Instead, the loss of the pregnancy had freed him to pursue other desires. Cruelly discarded and no longer needed, Jane had been set aside for his military career.

She pondered whether he supposed that a woman could so effortlessly recover from such heartbreak and betrayal. Since Matthew had ruined her life, having a civil conversation with the man was impossible. She would not give him the satisfaction of inching his way back into her existence in any fashion.

Silent tears dripped down her cheeks, and Jane wiped them away with the palm of her hand, angry with herself for even contemplating a good cry. She had mourned the loss of Matthew Rutland years ago and of their unborn child. She would no longer entertain any thought of him. Nothing needed to be resolved. Their business had concluded.

CHAPTER 9
A Song Out of Tune

A few days later, the date arrived to attend Lady Boggs's musical affair. She had no idea whether Neville or Matthew had received an invitation. Since she had taken a few days to recover and rearrange her thoughts, she felt confident that she could handle being in the same room with Matthew. To save herself from frustration, Jane planned to avoid him. If their paths did cross, she would be a woman of few words but polite.

Jane's goal remained the same before the presence of a particular individual pulled her off course. She wanted another male attachment for companionship and intimacy. Naturally, the usual rules would apply—love, accidental pregnancies, or marriage were not an option. As she remembered Lord Grisham, Jane hoped for his absence. Otherwise, he would be chasing her skirt all evening. Why she dangled the carrot of possibility before his nose she had no idea. It was a cruel thing to lead him on, but she had perfected cruelty long before Grisham came along.

The evening's event would be more intimate

in nature rather than a large attendance at the ball. Millicent planned to meet Jane upon arrival so that they could sit together during the performance. Jane wondered if a tenor or soprano would entertain or if the affair would have a small quartet of stringed instruments. Whatever the case, she wanted to enjoy herself and keep on the lookout for any new and exciting male attendees. A stab of remorse returned at having let Neville go too soon. How diverting it would be to see Matthew witness the two carrying on a disreputable affair behind closed doors.

To Jane's dismay, her punctuality to the event suffered delay. A carter overturned his haul, strewing coal over the roadway. As a result, she ended up in a long line of horse-drawn carriages, waiting for the road to clear. Rather than being early, it appeared she would now be at least fifteen minutes late. She hoped this incident was not a prelude to a miserable evening.

By the time she arrived, the preperformance gathering of attendees had ended. Millicent waited for her by the door before entering the music room. When she saw Jane, she grabbed her by the hand.

"Where have you been?"

"There was an incident on the road with an overturned carriage. It took some time before we were able to pass."

"Well, nevertheless, you're here now."

Jane touched her hair to make sure nothing

had fallen out of place and inhaled a breath to calm her jitters. Millicent stood, glancing at the audience who filled all the available chairs. Only two seats remained in the third row off to the left, so Jane led the way as her aunt followed behind. As soon as they reached the spot, Jane halted. There sat Matthew, speaking in a low voice, with his father. She had no other alternative but to sit next to him thanks to Millicent pushing her to do so before the performance began.

Jane's heart, for reasons not understood, thumped in her chest. She brought her hand to her throat thinking at any moment the pounding would stop. Whether it was from exertion, excitement, or nerves, she could not tell. A second later, Matthew turned his head, not realizing that she sat next to him. He jerked, and his eyes widened.

"Jane, I didn't see you come in," he remarked.

"Only a moment ago. Apparently, these were the only seats left," she said in an apologetic tone. "Otherwise, I would not be sitting here."

Suddenly his father took note of her presence. "Is that you, Lady Jane?" He looked around Matthew with astonishment written across his face.

"Yes, it's me, Sir Charles. I'm with my aunt Millicent."

"Oh, hello, Lady Whitmore," he remarked, adjusting his spectacles as if he needed to look again to make sure he was not dreaming. "Well, it's good to see you again."

Thankfully, the music began, and a tall and rather handsome man stood before the audience. He had ebony-black hair, a thin mustache, and dark eyes. Obviously, Lady Boggs had chosen a tenor for the entertainment who possessed more qualities than a good voice. When the first note left his lips, his talent mesmerized Jane. In fact, she became so engrossed in his performance that the reality of Matthew's presence faded away. Something of greater interest caught her eye.

She leaned over to Millicent and whispered in her ear. "Isn't he wonderfully talented?"

"And good-looking as well," Millicent added in response. "Lady Boggs didn't share that tidbit in her invitation."

"I wonder if he's married," Jane said in a voice far too loud. She saw Matthew turn his head in her direction, but she ignored him.

"Shush, Jane," Millicent scolded her. "People will hear." She gave her a little tap on her arm with her folded fan.

Jane decided to control her runaway musings and listen. The tenor sang various selections until an intermission occurred. She rose from her seat with the clear intent of finding out more about him. To her dismay, Sir Charles had other plans.

"Jane, how have you been?" he asked, pulling her attention in the other direction.

She glanced up at Matthew, who tilted his head slightly as if to ask her not to be rude to his father. Jane admitted upon a closer look that the man had aged quite a bit since she last saw him nine years prior. His hair had grayed, and there appeared a sense of frailty about his person. Remembering that he had been the one to pay Matthew's commission into service, she held no spot of endearment toward him. As far as she knew, Sir Charles never knew about the pregnancy.

"I have been well. And you?"

"Well, as good as any man my age," he replied with a broad smile. "Matthew told me that he ran into you earlier this week at the Westlake ball."

"Did he?" Jane replied, glancing up into Matthew's eyes. For some reason, he appeared tongue-tied or perhaps uncomfortable. The conversation prevented her from weaseling her way over to Lady Boggs, who stood talking to the tenor. "It is good to see you again, Sir Charles, but if you'll excuse me, I'd like to say a word of greeting to Lady Boggs."

Without glancing back at Matthew, Jane and Millicent left their places and walked over to congratulate their host on her triumphal choice of entertainment.

"Lady Whitmore and Lady Jane." She greeted them with a broad smile. "I would like to introduce you to Signore Vincenzo Romani from Florence."

"Your voice is divine," Millicent gushed.

Jane cocked her head and looked at her aunt, wondering if she too were making a bid for his attention. "Signore, I agree with my aunt. It is rare to hear such tone and clarity. The Italians are by far the best tenors on the Continent," she remarked, flashing a flirtatious smile.

"Thank you, my lady, for the compliment," he said, eyeing her with interest.

Jane batted her eyelashes, dangling the bait. "Are you in London visiting?"

"I have recently been cast in a new production at the Royal Opera House and shall be staying here for a few months," he replied.

"And how do you find our fine city? I'm sure it's much different from Florence," Jane remarked, already making her plans.

"Yes, yes, very different but a bit confusing at times."

"Well, you need a guide, perhaps, to help you navigate. I am more than happy to show you some more interesting landmarks and offer suggestions regarding our English cuisine." Jane could sense out of the corner of her eye Millicent's grin at her blatant bid to gain Vincenzo's attention.

"My wife would appreciate that very much," he replied. "She is anxious to visit the palaces and castles. Perhaps you could escort her next week upon her arrival."

"Your wife?" Jane's brow arched, and her stomach sank. Attempting to save herself from further embarrassment, she agreed. "I would be absolutely delighted," she replied.

Lady Boggs grinned in amusement. "Well, I think we are ready to hear more from the talented Signore Romani, don't you agree?"

"Yes, I do," Jane said with feigned enthusiasm. The audience started to retake their seats, and Jane sheepishly returned to the empty chair next to Matthew.

"It's nice of you to offer a tour to his wife," he chortled with a smirk.

She narrowed her eyes and glanced at his obvious amusement at her recent failure to entice. "How did you hear that from way back here?" she inquired.

"Oh, a little lip reading helps," he replied. Suddenly he leaned in and whispered in her ear. "Do you entertain married men, or are you only interested in the bachelor variety?"

Rather than answering straightaway, she thought about it for the moment. She had not taken a married man before, although she frivolously contemplated doing so when desperate. Nevertheless, she was not the mistress type. It bothered her, nonetheless, that Matthew wanted to know how far she would go for male companionship. Neville apparently hadn't shared with him her preferences. Instead of giving him a definite answer, she looked at him with a sly grin.

"What do you think I do?" she asked, staring at him boldly in the eyes.

"I suppose it doesn't matter what I think you do, Jane. It's your life to do as you will."

He turned his attention back to his father and began small talk until the performance started. Jane leaned back in her chair. Her earlier interest in the tenor waned, and now she was fully aware of who sat next to her. She sensed the heat of his body in the crowded room and leaned away slightly so that her arm did not graze across his side. Admittedly, he looked as handsome as he had earlier in the week, exuding his dominant male persona. To her chagrin, it began to tempt her mind to wander.

Matthew appeared oblivious to her presence as he watched the performance. Perhaps he had obtained an interest in the arts, when earlier in his life he showed little. It was too bad that Neville had not attended or she would have more diversion to keep her mind off Matthew.

After another half hour, the performance ended. Ecstatic that she could stand to her feet and move away from the radiating heat of Matthew Rutland, Jane was halted once again by the sound of his father's voice.

"Jane, might I have a word with you?" He reached across Matthew and tugged on her draping shawl, attempting to halt her departure.

"Father, I believe Jane is anxious to leave with her aunt," Matthew interjected.

"Well, we cannot let her go now, can we?" he protested. "Jane, I wish to invite you to Rutland Park next week. We are having a small dinner party, and it would be nice to have you in attendance."

A rush of panic shot through her veins, causing her to stumble over her words.

"Well, I . . . Well, I am flattered, Sir Charles, by your invitation."

"Then you will come. The dinner is on Friday eve of next week."

Millicent stood, silently watching the exchange, apparently not wishing to rescue her from the invitation. Hesitantly, Jane glanced up at Matthew, whose eyes showed a hint of despair as well. Jane had not the impudence to offend his father. The invitation must have been a surprise to Matthew as well.

"Yes, that would be convenient," she replied. "What time?"

"Dinner is at eight o'clock, but do come well before then in the late afternoon." He paused for a moment. "In fact, why don't you plan on spending the night with us? It will be a long carriage ride back to London in the dead of night, and I wouldn't wish any mishap to occur."

"Spend the night?" Her brow arched.

Matthew shifted in his chair, obviously uncomfortable with his father's bid to keep her there longer. It would have been much more convenient if they met here in London for dinner. Instead, he asked her to take a thirty-mile trip to Rutland Park. Suddenly, Matthew spoke a word of encouragement.

"It would please my father, Jane, if you would agree to the arrangement," he said with a pleading look in his eye.

"Very well. I shall plan to spend the evening and return to London the next morning."

"Excellent. It is all settled then," his father remarked with a broad smile.

Sir Charles looked at his son and smiled as if he possessed ulterior motives behind the invitation. Jane pondered the possibility and knew that was probably the case. The poor man was sorely misguided if he thought anything would come of it.

"I bid you good evening," she said, nodding at them both. Millicent walked to the door, and Jane followed behind with a sense of dread for having accepted the invitation.

"Are you sure about this, Jane?" Millicent said in a low voice, grabbing her arm.

"It's just a dinner party. Others will be in attendance," she replied, shaking off the possibility that anything else would come of it. "Don't worry about me. I will be fine." She hoped to God she would.

Chapter 10
∽ The Inconvenient Dinner Party ∽

While Jane's carriage made its way to Rutland Park, a myriad of memories flooded back. Matthew's estate lay five miles from her childhood home. She had not visited for over a year because she was not particularly close to her father. Even though he gave her an ample allowance, they led their lives separate from one another. Her father, a retired lawyer and second son of an earl, had inherited the earldom five years ago upon the death of his elder brother. Lord Cavanagh had his pursuits and circle of friends. The estate kept him occupied, as well as his love of horses and women.

They were not very different from one another in that regard. Jane's father had never remarried after her mother's death. Jane had a governess who, along with her aunt, was one of the female influences in her young life. Her father maintained a respectable distance, leaving her upbringing to others. Various women came and went as his lovers, and as a result, Jane was eager to leave home. When she met Matthew after her coming out, everything appeared to fall into place. Her father gave permission for her to wed, unaware that she was pregnant at the time.

Regrettably, life had other plans. When she began to profusely bleed, the family surgeon had been called. She eventually miscarried, at which time her father discovered her fallen state. Not pleased with her behavior, it placed a strain upon their relationship. A month later, Matthew left, and Jane went to live with her aunt Millicent to recover. She remained in London and never returned home.

As the years passed, Jane became increasingly independent, experiencing relationships one after the other. Already ruined by Matthew, she had no qualms allowing men to seduce her. After all, her weakness with Matthew had ruined her, anyway. There was nothing left of value to save for a future husband.

Each time she lay with another man, she enjoyed the pleasure and became less inhibited. Jane pondered if her lack of morals had been a way of punishing herself for what had happened. Unable to comprehend her motivations, she supposed it a mystery of the human mind that could not be solved. Jane threw away her scruples, garnered a scandalous reputation, and hardened her heart. Men became her entertainment and toys, and without an ounce of empathy, she discarded them when bored.

As the carriage approached Rutland Park,

Jane made a difficult decision before disembarking. For the sake of Matthew's father, who probably knew nothing about her current life, she would temper her behavior while staying in their home. As far as Matthew was concerned, she would be cordial but guarded.

Upon her arrival, a footman took the small bag she had packed for the overnight stay. Matthew met her at the door, acting pleased to see her. A warm smile brightened his face. He gave a slight bow, and she a small curtsy, which had been the first pleasantry exchanged between them that met social protocol.

"I sincerely hope that you had an agreeable trip," he remarked.

"I had forgotten how long it would be," Jane admitted. "I feel a bit bounced around from the country roads." She heard voices drift from the sitting room, recognizing one very distinct tone. "Don't tell me Neville is here," she asked, narrowing her eyes at Matthew. A mischievous grinned brightened his face.

"Well, it's a dinner party, and he's my friend, so yes, Neville is here."

"Good Lord," she moaned. "When I think I've had enough of the man, he shows up wherever I go like a shadow following me."

"You should know he has a lady with him," Matthew announced with a twinkle in his eye.

"You've got to be kidding me." Jane gasped in astonishment, thinking he had brought a guest to see if she would be jealous. "This I must see." As they entered the sitting parlor, Neville jumped to his feet.

"Well, if it isn't Lady Jane," he quipped, bowing at the waist. "Matthew told me to expect your arrival, but I could barely believe you would accept his invitation."

"I accepted the invitation of his father," she clarified. She glanced around the room and to her horror saw Lord Grisham sitting at a table, playing a game of cards with Sir Charles. Could it get any worse?

A young woman rose to her feet and stood next to Neville, brandishing a friendly smile. She appeared no older than eighteen years of age, looking very innocent. Her hair was golden like the color of wheat, her complexion rosy, and her frame petite. A youthful attractiveness radiated in her bearing.

"Hello, Lady Jane. I'm Neville's sister, Susan."

Neville had never mentioned a sister, and Jane immediately wondered why she had attended the party. She glanced at Matthew, who gazed warmly at the young woman. Naturally, Jane wondered if Neville was attempting to play matchmaker for Matthew, the idea of which she found dreadfully disturbing.

"It's a pleasure to make your acquaintance," Jane replied, eyeing her a bit closer. When she did, Jane's heart sank as the memory of her own eighteen-year-old life flooded back. Would

Matthew seduce this young creature as he had once done to her? Her brow furrowed with worry that he might consider her a candidate for marriage. "I wasn't aware that you had a sister," Jane glibly commented to Neville.

"She's just come out," Neville replied proudly. "Now that she's old enough, I saw no harm in bringing her to the dinner party to meet new people."

Jane attempted to remain cordial, hiding her underlying annoyance. "Miss Berkshire, I'm sure you've been busy this season at other functions. Any luck in your search for a husband?" Jane expressed her curiosity if someone else perhaps caught her eye.

The young girl giggled. "I'm afraid not but am hopeful. If not this season, perhaps the next."

Her eyes shifted over to Matthew, revealing her youthful infatuation for an older man. Neville smirked, and Jane surmised that he planned to push Susan upon Matthew. While Jane mulled over the disturbing possibilities, Sir Charles and Lord Grisham greeted her.

"Jane, so glad you came. Are you acquainted with Lord Grisham?" Sir Charles asked.

"Yes, we have met at other social functions," she replied. She gave a quick curtsy to them both.

"Lady Jane, I'm not sure if you have met my son Percy. He's recently engaged to Miss Boggs," Lord Grisham said. His demeanor toward her was respectful and guarded.

With all the upsetting introductions a moment ago, Jane had missed the young couple's presence in the large sitting room. Percy stood with Rose at his side, who Jane recognized. Daniella would be the next to announce an advantageous pairing at the gossip mill, and Jane was happy that she had successfully matched her daughter.

"Miss Boggs, how wonderful to see you," she began. "Congratulations to you both."

"Thank you, Lady Jane."

"Pleasure," Percy said, glancing over at his father with a smirk on his face.

Jane's heart sank at the thought that Lord Grisham had perhaps told him that he wished to be her next companion.

"Pleasure is all mine," Jane replied.

She wondered who else might come to the dinner party, but as the afternoon wore on, no other guests arrived. She settled into superficial conversations, occasionally taking note of Matthew's interaction with Susan. The young lady obviously had her eyes set upon the mature colonel, which distressed Jane. To her surprise, they both headed outdoors for a walk in the garden together. Jane swiftly attached herself to Neville.

"Do you think it wise to allow your sister to leave in the company of Matthew unchaperoned?" She clutched her fan in agitation, wanting to wallop Neville for allowing it to happen.

"I trust him," he calmly replied. "He's known Susan since she was a child, for heaven's sake." Neville dismissed her concerns.

"Your sister appears enamored. Does she hope to gain his affections?" Jane kept her eyes upon the veranda door, waiting for their return.

"Why Jane," Neville rebuked her jokingly. "If I did not know any better, I would surmise you are exhibiting a touch of jealousy."

"Jealousy?" Jane glanced sharply at him. "Why would I be jealous of anything Matthew does?"

"Because of unfinished business," Neville replied. He brandished a quirky grin.

"As I told you before, everything between us finished nine years ago. Why must you continue to poke at me about the past? I find it most annoying."

Jane flipped open her fan and wildly waved it in front of her face to ward off the blush filling her cheeks. Neville's annoying insinuations riled her. She grabbed his hand, pulled him to his feet.

"Come with me," she ordered. "I need some fresh air." Jane dragged him out the veranda door, anxious to know what Susan and Matthew were doing. Her actions incited Percy and Rose to follow, which had not been her intention.

"Do you mind if we join you?" Percy asked, taking Rose by the hand. "I could use a stroll before dinner."

Jane rolled her eyes at another obstacle

tagging along. It was not long before she spotted Matthew with Susan, standing by a small pond covered with lily pads. Thankfully, Percy and Rose meandered away in another direction. At first glance, the gardens were beautiful, and the aroma of flowers filled Jane's nostrils. She wrapped her arm around Neville's in a wicked ploy of her own.

"Does this mean you want me back?" he whispered. "I wouldn't mind."

"I haven't decided," she teased in return, flashing a disingenuous smile.

"I sense I'm being used again," he said in a melancholy tone. "Go ahead. I have not the strength to deny you anything you need."

Jane did not reply to his comment. Instead, she halted a few feet away from Matthew and noted that Susan's face appeared flushed. Surprised at their arrival, Matthew retreated from his position close to Susan, branding a sheepish expression on his face.

"Neville and I thought we would enjoy a moment outdoors as well. Didn't we, dear?" Jane said, tugging at Neville's arm.

"Yes. Jane suddenly became inspired to get a breath of fresh air and dragged me out the door." Neville smirked and gave Matthew a knowing glance for why they arrived. Matthew's eyes shifted toward Jane while she exhibited a less-than-friendly glance at Susan. The fresh air that whirled around the foursome in a gentle breeze suddenly ceased. Jane felt the heat of the afternoon sun bearing down upon her along with a mysterious rising temperature in the core of her stomach. The sight of Matthew and Susan together ignited an unexplainable possessiveness. She knew at that instant if she could not have Matthew, no other woman would either.

"Susan, walk with me," she said, dropping Neville's arm. "You must tell me about all the festivities you have enjoyed this season."

She reached out and grabbed Susan's hand, pulling her in the opposite direction of the two men. Slightly reluctant to leave Matthew, Susan glanced at him, flashing a helpless expression. Eventually, she relented to being dragged away and walked side by side as Jane led her down a pebbled path.

Jane dared not glance over her shoulder at the two men lest she witness their displeasure in her wicked ploy of interference. A sigh escaped her lungs, having successfully parted the two.

Chapter 11
~ Multiple Schemes ~

Colonel Rutland was no stranger to military tactics. After all, his nine years in service and numerous battles had taught him well. Military maneuvers in warfare held one purpose—to defeat the adversary by weakening their decision making through shock and distraction. Of course, he did not consider any of the present company his enemy. They were friends and acquaintances of various degrees, but each had an agenda.

Neville, for example, had shown up at Rutland Park with his younger sister in tow. When they extended the invitation to dinner, there had been no mention of bringing a guest. Instead, he took it upon himself to do so anyway. Susan, just out this season, was young and beautiful. Matthew had known her since the time she played with dolls but never considered her wife material. Neville, apparently, thought it a clever tactic to observe how he would react to her presence. Although Matthew didn't have the opportunity to pressure him for his motives behind the move, he realized that Neville had something up his sleeve. He wanted to either provoke him to find interest in his sister or provoke Jane to jealousy or some other emotion.

Then there was his dear father, who without Matthew's prodding had decided on a dinner party unexpectedly after seeing Jane at Lady Boggs's musical gathering. From that moment forward, his father had spoken about how lovely Jane looked and his surprise that she remained unwed. Matthew easily saw through his ploy to throw them together again in a social situation in the hopes that old sparks might reignite. Sir Charles had kept a fond spot in his heart for Jane, expressing disappointment at the breaking of their engagement nine years ago. Matthew never confessed to him the unborn child they lost through miscarriage.

Then there was Lord Grisham, the chubby, baldheaded man who drooled over Jane, wanting to be the next pick in a long line of men. It frankly irked Matthew to think that she would see anything in the man or ever entertain him in bed for that matter. Nonetheless, Grisham tagged along with his son Percy and Rose Boggs, acting as a chaperone. Matthew's father often played cards with the man, and they had a somewhat cordial relationship. Hopefully that was all Grisham would do the rest of the evening, play cards and not play Jane.

Susan, on the other hand, obviously entertained a youthful admiration for Matthew. Even though he was twelve years her senior, she apparently admired him for his heroism on the battlefield, among other things. Neville obviously used her and did not seem to care to protect her from disappointment. Matthew did not wish to break the young girl's heart and determined to be cordial but careful not to inspire any amorous affections.

Then there was Jane—beautiful Jane—the woman who took the breath away of every male in the room, including him. He watched her worried glint over his interaction with Susan and her devious ploy to use poor Neville to poke him in return. Matthew recognized she played a game as soon as she swooped in like a hawk and ambushed his walk in the gardens with Susan. The woman had not spent any time in the military, but she surely knew how to win her own battles.

As he considered everyone's strategy at a simple dinner party, Matthew formed his maneuver as well. As he observed Jane drag Susan yards away, walking farther into the garden and farther from him, he decided to engage in his own offensive move.

"Neville, go rescue your sister and take her back indoors," he ordered as if he were talking to one of his men on the battlefield. "I need a word with Lady Jane." He narrowed his eyes in her direction, viewing the rays of the afternoon sunshine through the fabric of her skirt.

"Irksome, isn't she?" Neville noted with sarcasm. "Frankly, I think it irks her that Susan wants your attention and Jane worries you want hers."

Matthew's head spun in Neville's direction and shot him a disgruntled glare. "You brought her just for that purpose, didn't you? You wanted to elicit some sort of reaction from Jane." He hesitated for a moment, considering the full purposes behind the maneuver. "And from me, for that matter."

"And what if I did?" Neville shrugged, walking away and heading for his sister. "What are friends for?"

Matthew watched as he approached the two ladies, spoke a few words, and eventually lead Susan back into the house. Jane cast a glance at Matthew, and he marched to battle, striding assuredly in her direction. She flipped open her fan and began her silent indications. Matthew had been out of practice interpreting fan flipping signals for some time and possessed no clue what she attempted to convey.

"Why did you have Neville snatch Susan away from me?" she complained, quickly closing the fan.

Her impetuous snapping shut of the fan had something to do with jealousy, he remembered. The look on Jane's face and her actions elicited a sly curl of his lips. Matthew concluded that in the next few minutes he needed to choose his words and movements carefully to take her by surprise.

"I had a sudden urge to speak with you in private," he remarked in a steady tone.

"About what?" She flipped her fan back open and rested it on her chest.

For the life of him, he could not remember that maneuver either. The fan became an instrument of irritation. He wanted to speak plainly, not by some odd method of communication that kept a person from honest conversation. With difficulty, he softened the tone of his voice.

"Walk with me, Jane. It's been some time since we have spoken of anything beyond simple social pleasantries." He offered his arm, and she looked at it for a moment before taking it. With another gesture on his part, she finally obliged and closed the fan to let it dangle from her wrist.

The pebbled pathway of their gardens went for some length, leading to an old garden maze. When Matthew courted her as a youth, they had enjoyed flitting about the confusing twists and turns. Memories of the past flooded his mind. Oddly, he had an urge to see what her reaction would be, because amidst one of the dead-end turns is where he had taken her virginity. It was a bold and perhaps insensitive move on his part, but he needed to know what emotions it would elicit.

"There's something I've meant to say," she admitted. Her kind voice had a tone of empathy. "I wanted to express to you, Matthew, my sincere condolences on the loss of your wife and son."

Unaware that she had been privy to that information, it took him by surprise. Nevertheless, he sensed the sincerity in her expression and accepted it with grace. "Thank you, Jane." Rather than asking further questions that would open painful memories, she let the matter rest.

"How is your father?" Matthew asked out of curiosity.

"My father is the same emotionally detached man as always, pursuing his own interests and pleasures."

"Do you see him often?"

"Rarely. We have nothing in common," Jane quipped.

Matthew said nothing further, remembering her disappointment over their poor relationship.

"I left home and went to live with my aunt after your departure," she added. "Millicent is more of a parent to me than he has ever been." They took a few more steps toward the hedges of the maze. "Your father must be proud of you, Matthew. Coming home as a decorated war hero is an accomplishment."

"I'm happy to be back alive," he admitted, "and nothing more."

They continued walking, and Jane appeared oblivious to the location. "Do you remember the maze?" he asked, with a twinkle in his eyes. "I recall our frequent lighthearted runs, losing track of each other inside the rows of hedges."

Jane looked but did not react with any recollection, or if she did, she hid it behind her pleasant countenance. "It's been so long ago," she admitted, looking curiously at the entrance.

It took a few moments of pondering before Jane's features soured. Her gazed shifted to Matthew warily. "I recall a very distinct portion of the maze, now that you mention it."

"It's still there," Matthew replied. "I don't suppose you would care to revisit?"

His suggestion did not sit well with her, and she dropped her arm from his in haste. "I don't believe I care to revisit it," she solemnly said, taking a step back.

"Your aunt clearly remembers the incident. In fact, Lady Whitmore gave me a piece of her mind at the ball," he divulged, hoping that it would change her mind.

Jane looked at him, cockeyed. "She did? In what sense?" The tone of her voice turned tense and her stance uneasy.

"Well, if you must know," he said, lowering his head, "she thinks I am to blame for your choices in life."

"That's an odd thing to say," she snapped. "My aunt has never expressed to me her disappointment in my decisions." Jane huffed, revealing her agitation. "If anything, Millicent and her friends praise me for having chosen a path none of them had the bravery to pursue." Jane lifted her chin with an air of pride. "In fact, they admire me."

"They deem you a hero too?" Matthew said in a mocking tone.

"A hero in what sense?"

"Leaving victims strewn across the battlefield of love," he said, knitting his brows together in a frown.

"I wouldn't put it that way," she dismissed him, taking another step away.

"Even Neville seems to think that I am to blame for your current life choices," he announced, observing her for a reaction.

"Neville," she balked. "What right does he have to comment on my choices in life when he readily partook of my body night after night without complaint?" She flipped open her fan and began rapidly swinging it in front of her face to cool her reddened cheeks.

Matthew found no amusement in her answer. If anything, he felt awful. Whatever he did to her nine years ago had left an indelible mark on her heart. Perhaps he had been responsible for the way she turned out. Instead of remaining as the young lady he once admired, quiet and shy, she had transformed into a hellion of a woman. By all accounts, Jane should be married, with children around her feet. Instead, she remained single with men applying for a place in her bed. In all honesty, the woman Jane had changed into distressed him to the core.

"Come with me," he ordered in a stern voice,

grabbing her hand and pulling her into the maze.

Surprisingly, without protest, she followed. After years of running through it as a boy and a young man, he knew every twist and turn like the back of his hand. He led her to the three-sided dead end, with six-foot-tall green hedges on each side. He halted, and Jane glanced around, lowering her eyes to the grassy spot on which he had taken her innocence.

"Why did you bring me here?" Her eyes narrowed at him in suspicion.

"To ask for your forgiveness," he humbly said.

"There is nothing to forgive," she argued, scrunching her lips together. "I knew exactly what I was doing when I lay with you, and I did so willingly."

"But if I hadn't of seduced you, Jane, things would have turned out different."

"You mean if I hadn't gotten pregnant and lost the baby? That's rubbish," she protested. "Besides," she seethed. "You never loved me as I loved you. Our marriage would have been a catastrophe, consisting of my craving for you and your cold indifference. If you had settled for me instead of the military, you would have been miserable and made me miserable too." She whacked his arm in anger with her closed fan.

Matthew had had enough of that damnable accessory. He ripped the cord off her wrist, grabbed the fan, and threw it over the hedge to the other side.

"What did you do that for?" she screeched. "You . . ."

Without another thought, he pulled her into his arms, encircled his mouth on hers to shut her up, kissing her ardently to halt any protest. At first, Jane fought him with a few weak punches of her fist upon his chest, but when he tightened his hold around her waist, she swiftly relented to his advances.

At last he had won a small battle but not the war. He realized at that moment, as he tasted the sweet nectar of her lips, that he wanted to reclaim Jane in some fashion.

Chapter 12
～ Ambushed and Captured ～

The colonel had just ambushed her emotions at the same location he had nine years prior. Crushed in his embrace, he swallowed her frame in his arms, making it impossible for her to wiggle her way out. His lips pressed against her with such force that she opened her mouth. A second later, he entered her with his tongue, drinking her in as if he were dying of thirst. Jane realized that it had been some time since he had enjoyed a woman.

Initially, she balled her fist against him but found the action futile. He wanted her and perhaps had planned to seduce her on the same grassy spot he had done before. The question loomed before her—would she allow him to do so? He was the first to breach her maidenhood, which had led her to a long list of those who followed afterward.

As he continued to kiss her, barely taking a breath, her mind whirled like a dust devil of mixed emotions. He stirred a dormant place in her heart she wished would remain untouched.

Although it tempted her to express an ounce of high regard for Matthew, he lacked the power to change her determination to be a free woman of choice. As he aggressively devoured her, Jane responded like any other woman with sexual needs. Her body became moist, yearning for his entrance, leaving in her an aching need for satisfaction. As a result, she returned his kisses with equal enthusiasm.

At last their lips parted, and they gasped for breath. Matthew had perfected the art of kissing since their mouths last touched. With precision, he held her firmly to his body so she sensed his erection, and used his hands to caress precisely in the right places. In fact, his male attraction had increased tenfold in every way. He was strong, virile, and had left behind the boyish youthful look. It was difficult not to gaze at him without a hint of admiration in her eyes. He had matured into a handsome male specimen, just the type she was seeking for her next tryst. Jane remained cautious, though, until she fully understood his intentions behind the amorous assault.

"Why did you do that?" she asked as he stood there with an air of conquest on his face.

"Because I've wanted to do that for some time now," he admitted.

"And what do you hope to gain by that kiss, if anything? My body or my affections?"

He took a step back but kept his hands on her waist. "I haven't decided," he readily admitted, looking torn. He narrowed his eyes at her, studying the features of her face. "You are a delectable woman, Jane, and obviously, many men want your body. I'm no different, honestly, and wouldn't mind ravishing you myself."

"Hmmm," she mused aloud, eyeing him like a delectable piece of candy. "I do have an opening for a new companion and could accommodate you, but it would have to be on my terms." She grinned at him, batting her eyelashes. "Would you consider the arrangement?"

He bolted a hearty laugh and dropped his hands from her waist. "I've never had a woman proposition me as you have just now." Amused at her offer, he stood, eyeing her breasts as if they were ripe melons. Eventually, his eyes lazily crawled up her frame and met her gaze. "And what would I gain out of this liaison?" he asked with an arched brow of skepticism.

"I can tell you straight away that if you are looking for love, continue your search elsewhere. I gave up on that useless emotion a long time ago."

"I gathered," he replied, his eyes darkening. "It's a shame, frankly, but if you don't wish my love, then I can accommodate that request."

"But if you need companionship and a bit of pleasure, I'm your lady." She went to look for her fan and glanced around. "Damn it," she spat out. "Where's my fan?"

"Over the hedge." He snickered. "No need to

be coy with your signals. I prefer the use of concise conversation to convey a point."

As she stood there looking at him, her body continued to ache. "What is your answer, Colonel?" Jane pressed. "Do you wish to visit my bed or not?" Her wicked bid burst from her lips, and suddenly Neville entered her mind. She wondered if this would drive a wedge between his friendship with Matthew. "You don't think that would bother Neville, do you?" she asked with a concerned frown. "I wouldn't wish to cause trouble between the two of you."

"Neville has given me his blessing to bed you," he announced. "He knows it's been a while, and he said you'd be the perfect lady to help with my lack of physical intimacy."

"Oh, has he?" Jane replied, pulling her lips to the side at the rascal's ploy. "I'm surprised he hasn't asked for a threesome."

Her statement caused Matthew to frown. A second later, he pulled her hard toward his body and held her captive and unable to move in his arms.

"No threesomes," he growled. "Just you and me."

She studied the determined glint in his eyes for a moment and set her conditions. "I don't do long-term relationships," Jane announced, bending her head back and looking at him as he towered above her. "And I have rules."

"What kind of rules?"

"Rules about safeguarding my person," she said, casting a threatening gaze. "I don't wish to be impregnated, especially by you, again."

"I see," he replied.

If he did not agree to her terms, Jane decided she would walk in the other direction. As she felt his manhood harden against her pelvis, she knew that he wanted her at any cost. Admittedly, Jane wanted him. Perhaps it was for old times' sake, or maybe it was because she had been starving for intimacy and satisfaction the past weeks. Whatever the reason, she wanted to lay with Matthew and wondered if he had learned how to satisfy a lady by now.

"So, Colonel, do you agree?"

"Agree."

"And you accept the rules?"

"Rules accepted."

"Good. I look forward to our first encounter, but it won't be here in the grass by the hedges," Jane replied, eyeing the ground underneath her feet.

"Fine," he grumbled. "Your place or mine?"

"I have an agreeable bedchamber," she offered. "Let's use mine."

"Will next week be convenient?"

"Next week will do. Tuesday, at eight o'clock in the evening. If that conflicts with another engagement on your calendar, I can do Wednesday."

"Tuesday it is," he replied, straight-faced.

"Should I bring wine?"

"I prefer champagne. Don't forget your English riding coats or French letters, whatever you prefer."

Matthew smirked. "I'm sure we can think of other things to do if my memory lapses in that regard."

"You appear to be an expert with your tongue," she seductively drawled. "Do you know how to use it elsewhere?"

He lifted her chin with his finger and then breathed heavily in her ear. "I'm sure you taste delectable all over."

His tone sent a shiver down her spine. "Shall we return to join the others?" Jane suggested, pulling away from his hard erection. It had become increasingly difficult not to lay with him on the inviting grass beneath their feet. "It appears we have concluded the contractual aspects of the arrangement."

"Do you wish to get it in writing?" he asked.

"A verbal contract will do," she replied. "You can let go now."

He released her and offered his arm to lead her out of the maze. For some odd reason, she remembered the correct twists and turns. A part of her wanted another kiss, but there would be plenty of time for that in the future. As they returned indoors, everyone glanced at them curiously.

"We were about to send out a search party,"

Neville joked, eyeing her quizzically.

"I apologize for the delay," Matthew said, dropping Jane's arm. "We were reminiscing about old times."

Jane noted that Susan's bright countenance had dulled. Perhaps Neville had set her straight and told her not to set her sights on Matthew.

Rather than attach herself permanently to the colonel the entire evening, causing a scene, she walked over and started conversing with Percy and Rose. Matthew, on the other hand, remained in the company of Susan and Neville, exchanging pleasantries.

The afternoon slipped away until the dinner hour. Everyone appeared to delight in each other's company, and luckily, Lord Grisham behaved himself the entire evening, not trying to approach her alone on any occasion. After supper, they returned to the parlor to spend their remaining time together. Susan played the pianoforte and sang a beautiful piece, having the voice of an angel.

Around eleven o'clock, Lord Grisham, Percy, and Rose departed. When the clock chimed midnight, Jane felt exhausted. "I hope you don't mind, Sir Charles, but I'd like to retire. It has been a long day."

"Yes, yes, of course, young lady," he said. "Neville and Susan, your rooms are ready too if you wish."

"Thank you. I'm ready to call it a night as

well," Neville replied. "Come along, Susan."

Susan gave her regards. "Good night to you all, and thank you for the wonderful dinner, Sir Charles." She gave a curtsy, smiled at Matthew, ignored Jane, and followed Neville out the parlor door.

"I'll show you to your room," Matthew said, offering his arm to Jane.

"Good night, Sir Charles," Jane said.

"Good night. Pleasant dreams."

Neville and Susan had disappeared upstairs, and Matthew escorted her up the dark staircase, holding a small lighted candelabra. Rutland Park's interior was dark, with old tapestries hanging on the walls and large portraits of dead ancestors. The stairs, covered in a deep red carpet with a mahogany banister, led to a landing with a long corridor of rooms. They crept down the hall, and Matthew stopped at the fourth door.

"This is your room, Lady Jane."

The candlelight flickered in his eyes and surrounded the two of them in an aura of desire. Jane studied him quietly for a few seconds, contemplating their joining. Perhaps she should question her sanity for suggesting their involvement or even examine her motives for doing so. The bitterness in her heart had been there for a long time, but having Matthew back in her life gave her a choice. She could toy with his emotions as he had done to her, or she could be foolish and allow her heart freedom. As she thought about it, she seriously doubted that anyone could soften her hardened soul. All she cared about was the physical satisfaction. Besides, she had no indication that Matthew experienced any emotions either except the lust for a woman's body. Why should he suddenly fall in love with her now? He certainly didn't care enough nine years ago.

Matthew reached behind her and turned the doorknob, opening the bedchamber for her to enter.

"Well, good night, Colonel Rutland," she said, smiling at him. "I shall not give you a kiss good night, as that act was not covered in our arrangement."

"Understandable," he noted. "We should keep our agreement and nothing more."

Jane backed into the room and took a single candle from the candelabra. "If you don't mind, I need one to light mine."

"Good night, Jane," Matthew said in a noncommittal tone. "Breakfast is at eight o'clock."

"Good night." She closed the door, leaned against it, and closed her eyes. Oh God, she wanted to ravage him, but she would have to wait until Tuesday.

She walked over to the candle on the fireplace mantel and lit it with a few others. It would be a long night in a single bed.

Chapter 13

∽ A Nighttime Visitor ∽

Exhausted, Jane fell into a deep sleep. She did not toss and turn to contemplate the week ahead. Her dreams were pleasant, and her body comfortable until a few hours later.

"Jane," whispered a voice. "Jane, wake up."

The voice sounded like a buzz in her ear rather than someone whispering her name. All she knew was that she wanted to swat it away, so that is what she did. Her hand flew up into the air, and it whacked something hard.

"Ouch!"

The undeniable voice of Neville pulled her rudely from her slumber, and she shot up in bed. He sat there covering his nose with his hand.

"Why did you hit me?" he complained. "It feels like you broke my nose."

She rubbed her eyes and glowered at him. "You deserve it for waking me up in the dead of night."

The moonlight streamed through the parted curtains, illuminating the interior enough for her to see his features. "What time is it?"

"Three," he said, still rubbing his nose.

"What are you doing in my room, Neville?"

"I wanted to talk to you."

"At this hour?" she complained. "Couldn't this wait until the morning?" Jane sat up and glared at him, sitting on the edge of her bed. She pulled the covers up to her chest and yawned. He was clad in a nightshirt that was open down the front, exposing his chest. It was the last thing she needed to see—naked skin.

"Well, then talk and let me get back to sleep."

"I'm cold," he complained. "Can I crawl under the covers with you?"

"No," she emphatically replied.

"Why not? I'm shivering," he said with chattering teeth.

"Because I'm naked, that's why." She dropped the covers and exposed her breasts and then pulled the blanket back up.

"Good God, woman!" Neville reached out to touch her breast, and she walloped his hand.

"Behave." When she noticed that his teeth were chattering, she gave in and threw back the covers enough for him to crawl in. "All right, you big baby. I wouldn't want to be responsible for you catching your death of cold."

His eyes widened at the opportunity, and he quickly slipped underneath, pulling the blanket over him. Jane scooted over to the far side of the bed, avoiding physical contact.

"We could cuddle. That will warm me up." He chuckled.

"No, cuddling," she adamantly replied. "Now say what you have to say and let me get back to sleep."

Neville eyed her naked shoulders, and she purposely pulled the sheet over herself to hide her nudity. The last thing she needed was a man clawing at her body and Matthew finding out.

"What's going on between you and Matthew?"

"Nothing," she said, shrugging off the comment.

"I don't believe you," he replied.

"We came to an arrangement," she admitted, yawning again.

"What kind of arrangement?"

"Why don't you ask Matthew instead of me? I'm sure he wouldn't mind you crawling into his bed at three o'clock in the morning."

"Very funny," he grinned. "Tell me what's going on."

"I will tell you, but I don't want you talking to Matthew about it. It's our private affair."

He hesitated to agree, but his curiosity won the argument. "All right. I won't speak of it to him."

"He wants to be my companion, so I agreed."

"What?" His voice echoed in the room.

"Shush! Do you want everyone to hear you? That's all I need is for someone to find you in bed with me."

"Was that your idea or his?"

"I suggested it, and he agreed to it." She recalled Matthew's earlier words. "Besides, he said you offered me up for comfort."

"I did, but I didn't think you would take him on based on your past with the man." He fell into a digestive silence, frowning at the thought.

"Are you bothered by it?" Jane asked, softening the tone of her voice. "I don't want to hurt you, Neville. You're a nice man, and we had a good go of it."

"I'm not jealous or hurt, Jane, only concerned. You're out to destroy him, aren't you?"

"No," she answered half-heartedly. "We are both available for a tryst, so I thought why not?"

"Liar," Neville spat out. In a surprise move, he flipped off the covers, swung his legs around the edge of the bed, and rose to his feet. "I don't like the idea of you doing to Matthew what you do to all men. And frankly, I question your motives in welcoming him to your bed."

"Well, I warned him and spelled out the rules. He's aware," Jane said, defending her actions. "I told him love, babies, and marriage were definitely not acceptable."

"You're going to hurt him to get back at you for something that happened nine years ago. The man is my friend, and I don't appreciate your plan of destruction."

Riled by his accusations, Jane wanted to stand

up and give Neville a piece of her mind. Unfortunately, her nakedness kept her in bed, wrapped in the blanket.

"He's perfectly capable of making his choices, as I am mine. He knows the risks, and I told him emphatically not to think any affection would come from the arrangement. It's purely companionship and physical intimacy, as it was between the two of us."

"No, as it was for *you*, Jane—until I fell in love with you like a damn fool." Neville headed for the door. "I should warn him like everyone warned me. Perhaps he'll take heed before it's too late."

"Where are you going?" she demanded.

"Back to my room," he grumbled. A second later, he opened the door and slipped out into the hallway.

"Good riddance," she said, lying back down. She plopped her head on the pillow and ruminated over the short and disagreeable conversation. Matthew knew exactly what he was getting himself into, and it was his responsibility to guard his heart—not hers.

After punching the pillow a few times with her fist to get comfortable, she buried her head in a soft spot and closed her eyes. Too bad it hadn't been Matthew who woke her up and crawled under the covers. Then she wouldn't have to wait until Tuesday.

Neville did not intend to keep quiet about Jane's plans. He headed downstairs well before the eight o'clock breakfast call and luckily found Matthew sitting at the table alone, having a cup of tea and reading the newspaper. He grabbed an empty chair to the left of him and sat down.

"We need to talk."

Matthew eyed him, lowering the paper to the tabletop. "Well, good morning to you too," he said. "You seem a bit rushed about something."

"Rushed isn't the word for it. How about incited, enraged, worried, and determined to talk you out of this harebrained idea of yours regarding Jane?"

"She told you, did she?" he frowned. "I hoped to keep that between the two of us."

"Well, I dragged it out of her, frankly, and am glad I did." Neville's mouth felt like a ball of dry cotton, so he poured himself a cup of tea and took a few sips before continuing. After drinking the refreshment, he calmed somewhat and spoke.

"Before I became involved with Jane, I had numerous other men approach me."

"About what?"

"They warned me about her ways, Matthew. Her use and abuse of the male population." Neville inhaled a deep breath and spewed out in one long sentence, "Do you have any idea whatsoever how she will shred you to pieces, leave you wounded, and step over you while you're bleeding to death from a broken heart?"

"I can imagine the woman is quite vicious when it comes to hurting men, but as you so aptly reminded me, Jane and I have unfinished business."

"Then I curse the moment I said that to you. Had I any indication you would decide to finish the business in bed with Jane, I would have told you otherwise. Don't you think that talking rather than strumming would be a safer choice?"

"Strumming? Really, Neville?" Matthew bellowed a laugh. Afterward, he looked calmly at his friend and attempted to allay his fears. "I'm going into this arrangement with my eyes wide open. I assure you." Matthew took a sip of tea and then continued. "Give me a little credit. I may have my own plans in the matter."

"What plans?"

"Well, first, to enjoy female comfort." He snickered. "After that, we'll see where it leads."

"It will lead to your destruction," Neville reiterated.

Matthew studied him for a moment. "Are you still in love with her? Tell me the truth."

"Not really," Neville admitted. "I'm ready to move on, though I still admire the woman, clothed and naked." He smirked, thinking about sharing her bed for a mere minute the evening before, but he was not about to tell Matthew.

"Then I have no hesitation in accepting her

proposal for an arrangement of convenience." As Matthew finished his words, his father entered the dining room. Behind him wandered in Susan, but Jane was absent.

"Good morning, everyone," Sir Charles said. "Did you have a good rest?"

"Yes, it was fine," Neville said half-heartedly.

"Well, the warmers are filled with breakfast. Take a plate and help yourself before you and your sister travel homeward."

Neville witnessed Jane wander into the room. She had dark circles under her eyes, and he wickedly felt glad she had lost some sleep, hopefully due to their conversation.

"Good morning," she said.

Neville nodded. Susan avoided her. Sir Charles smiled, and Matthew winked. As far as Neville was concerned, his friend was about to be eaten alive, and there was nothing he could do about it.

Chapter 14

ᗡ Keeping the Appointment ᗡ

Tardiness was not an option, so Matthew arrived at Jane's town house precisely at eight o'clock on Tuesday evening. Since the dinner party and Neville's heated warning, Matthew had taken time to reflect on their ensuing arrangement. When it came to matters of the heart, he had always proceeded with caution. It took time for him to become vulnerable to any woman. Even when he met Felicity, he had moved cautiously toward the altar. When he did, Matthew realized he possessed a dangerous weakness—he gave the totality of his soul when in love. As a result, the pain he suffered upon Felicity's death had been enormous. It had taken him too long to move beyond his loyalty even though she lay dead in a grave.

As a rational man, he had the good sense to guard his heart and intended to do so with Jane. Their kiss in the maze had perhaps taken him down a dangerous path that could lead nowhere. At that opportune moment, he had wanted her regardless of the consequences. Maybe the desire had been due to the guilt Millicent and Neville had heaped upon him in the past weeks. A broken heart and a woman scorned had become an unpleasant combination.

The more he thought about the possibility of captivating Jane's heart, the more difficult the challenge appeared. He was not the type of man who quit when faced with an obstacle. After all, he had led men into battle, for heaven's sake. It would take a battle of wits if that were his goal. He saw it as a matter of outmaneuvering her plans, being smarter than Jane's wiles, and capturing her heart in a surprise attack. The only difference here was that he was enjoying the spoils ahead of the conquest.

Like any man of conscience, however, Matthew did seriously consider that he would be wantonly using Jane's body for his own pleasure. He admired her beauty but hadn't fallen blindly in love just yet. His motives rose from curiosity and physical need. After all, she had offered herself, and since he had known her before, he justified accepting her proposition.

Regardless, as any gentleman should do, he wrestled with the guilt, knowing to take her with ulterior motives and for selfish pleasure was disrespectful. The more he thought about it, the easier it became to ignore the guilt since Jane had chosen not to respect herself when it came to giving her body to multiple men. After mulling over the morality of the situation until his brain hurt, he decided to forge ahead.

Matthew stood in front of her door, clutching a bottle of champagne in one hand, and his top hat in the other. With a hard rap of the knocker, it soon opened. He half expected a house servant to answer. Instead, Jane greeted him, obviously pleased by his punctual arrival from the smile on her face.

"I was expecting a stern butler on the other side," he smirked.

"No butler. I only employ a maid, but she does not live with me. It's difficult to do what I do, sharing my home with the hired help."

"I imagine so." Matthew stepped inside, and Jane closed the door behind him. "Champagne, my lady, as requested."

She took the bottle and read the label. "You have expensive tastes," she remarked. "And it's still chilled, no less."

"Only the best for you," he replied. Matthew glanced around his surroundings.

"Why don't you come into the parlor for a moment, and we'll have a few drinks before getting down to business."

After looking at her comfortable quarters, Matthew pointedly asked, "How do you support yourself if you are no man's mistress?"

"Well, I'm not a prostitute, if that's what you're thinking," she said, holding two crystal flutes. "Pop the cork while the bottle is still cool."

Matthew obliged, and with a big bang, it flew

across the room. They both laughed at its trajectory. He poured two glasses and then took a seat in a single chair. Jane sat in a small red settee across from him.

"You haven't answered my question," he reminded her.

"My father gives me an ample allowance. Since he has no sons or other relatives to inherit his estate, he keeps me well cared for as long as I keep in his good graces."

Matthew's brow rose. "Well, he's generous though not personable in his character."

"True," Jane remarked.

She took a sip of her champagne. "I am extremely grateful for his generosity in spite of our lukewarm relationship."

Matthew fell into a pondering silence, taking note of the pictures on the wall, the furniture, and the tastes that Jane expressed in the décor. The room was comfortable and inviting, illuminated with enough candlelight to create a relaxing atmosphere.

"So how does this work?" he asked, settling back in the chair. He dangled one hand over the rest and held his glass in the other, taking sips.

"What do you mean?"

"Your companionship with men, of course," he clarified. "Do we converse for an hour or two? Drink until we are overly relaxed? Or do men just arrive and drag you into your bedroom?" He flashed an impish grin.

"My dear, Matthew," she cooed like a pigeon. "You are quite amusing."

"Well, I admit I didn't sit down with Neville after our last conversation long enough to receive any tutoring on the intricacies of your relationships."

"That's exactly what it is, a companionship. I enjoy your company and get to know you. We occasionally attend social functions together or partake in activities we both enjoy. Then, as the mood allows, we also enjoy intimacy with one another behind closed doors."

"Doesn't it give people the suggestion that you are being courted?"

Jane burst out laughing. "With my reputation? Oh dear God, no."

She gulped the remainder of her champagne and held it out to him to fill again. Matthew obliged and filled her glass and topped off his, setting the bottle back down. Matthew sat quietly pondering, gazing at her as if he were solving a puzzle.

"It's existence then, between two people, with no particular goal to achieve," he concluded.

"Well, I do have expectations of achieving something," Jane replied coyly.

"Don't we both?" he remarked flatly. "I understand the parameters of this arrangement."

"Might I ask you a question?" Jane asked as her facial expression grew serious.

"You may."

"Tell me about your wife. How did you meet her, and how long were you married?" she paused for a second. "That is, if you don't mind me asking."

A slight uneasiness washed over Matthew as he frankly did not care to discuss his dead wife. He knew if Felicity came into his mind, and he decided to have a sexual encounter with Jane, guilt could interfere with his conscience. Of course, he had every right as a widower to pursue women again, but something deep inside remained when it came to Felicity.

"You appear distressed, Matthew. Are you not over your dead wife?"

He swiftly found offense in her question. "One does not get *over* a dead wife. One mourns the loss, but their memory and the love you shared remains in your soul."

Jane lowered her eyes, seemingly contrite for having touched a delicate spot. "I suppose that is true and apologize for my insensitive question."

Matthew knew why she did not understand the concept. "Do you ever get *over* the men you let go, or do you have no emotional attachment to them when you tire of their company?"

"I have no emotional attachment," she resolutely replied without hesitation. "Instead, I have a heart of stone so that I do not experience the need to get *over* anyone again," she said with a clenched jaw.

Jane doused the remainder of her champagne in one gulp, clearly agitated. After setting the glass down on a table, she fiddled with her skirt for a moment, withdrawing herself from the conversation. Her actions reminded Matthew of a cute rabbit, poking its head out from a burrow in the ground only to suddenly retreat once it sensed danger. He detected the initial peaceful atmosphere in the room diminish, and Matthew knew that he had to swiftly turn things around.

"I sense we are going about this all wrong," Matthew concluded, heaving a sigh. After drinking the remainder in his glass, he set it down next to Jane's empty flute. He rose to his feet and slipped onto the settee next to her, putting his arm around her shoulder. Her body relaxed at his touch, and he inhaled her delectable scent. "Your fragrance is pleasing," he remarked.

She lifted her eyes and looked at him with a softened facial expression. "I'm glad you approve."

"It has a trace of rose that tempts me to peel back the petals of a flower and examine the bud."

Her brow arched. "And what would you like to peel first, Colonel?" After her coy inquiry, Jane traced her index finger down the side of his face and then stopped at his lips. She leaned into him and gave him a sweet kiss that did nothing at all to arouse him. It might help if he rid her of the dress she wore for the evening. Frankly, he had barely taken notice of it, except that it was blue, the usual empire waist, short-sleeved, and low enough to see the rounding of her breasts. The skirt was fuller than women had worn a few years ago, but he hoped to soon see it pooled at her feet.

Gently, he let his hand slip down the center of her back, counting the buttons that guarded the bodice. Eight in a straight row led to a small tied sash just above her waist. He fingered it and pulled it loose, and Jane's eyes widened.

"One usually starts at the top and then works their way down. You'll never get me out of this dress with one slip of a ribbon." She smirked and reached toward his neck, fingering the knot of his white cravat. "You must be warm," she suggested, untying it and pulling it loose. His shirt lay open at the neckline, and she grinned approvingly.

After tossing the tie onto a nearby chair, Matthew undid the first button of her dress. "Yes, that does feel much better," he remarked. "I'm sure you must be a bit warm yourself." The first slipped through the eyelet quickly, then the second, third, fourth, fifth, sixth, seventh, and eighth. The fabric opened, revealing her bare back, and he slipped his hand across her skin, astonished at the smoothness of the petal he had plucked.

In response, Jane took both hands, grabbed the lapel of his frock coat, and pushed it off his shoulders. She tugged it down his arms and let it drop to the floor. Then she methodically unbuttoned the four buttons of his brocade waistcoat, releasing it entirely and then pushing it off his shoulders too. His white ruffled linen shirt draped loosely about his chest, and Jane slipped her hand between the openings and felt his skin. She closed her eyes, expressing pleasure at touching him. Starved for sexual gratification, it took no time for Matthew to become aroused as they kissed each other in anticipation.

"I don't enjoy contorted lovemaking on a small settee," Jane admitted, tugging at the waistband of his pants. "Perhaps we should relocate to my bedchamber."

Matthew rose to his feet and offered his hand, which Jane took, squeezing it in return. She stepped ahead, pulling him along to the staircase. When they reached the landing above, she let go, turned around, and motioned with her finger to follow her. A delightful grin lit up her face as he entered a candlelit garden of delight.

A sizable four-poster canopy bed sat in the middle of the room, appearing as the central object of Jane's bedchamber. The dark mahogany carved headboard contrasted against red silk damask fabric that draped down the four posts. A puffy mattress, covered in a white silk duvet, glistened from the light of the candles that illuminated the room. The scent of roses filled his nostrils.

"Did you bring anything else?" she asked. "I

keep a special drawer in the nightstand to store certain items when needed."

He did remember, but they were in the inside pocket of his frock coat strewn across the floor downstairs. "Not on my person. They are in my coat. Shall I get them?"

Jane walked toward him, turned around, and exposed her back. "No need, I have a small supply."

Matthew's hands pushed the dress off her shoulders, and he let them rest on the rounding of her upper arms. He kissed the back of her neck, allowing his fingers to explore. As he glanced at the comb that held her locks together, he pulled it out and let her dark curls cascade. They covered her bare skin, and she shook them loose. He needed to see more. As he pulled her dress downward, he was astonished to see that she wore nothing underneath. She giggled.

"I thought I would make it easy for you, so I dressed lightly this evening." Slowly, Jane turned around and let the dress pool at her feet. She took Matthew's hand and placed it on her rounded breast. "Yours to enjoy," she seductively invited. "Touch, taste, and be filled, dearest."

The young and shy eighteen-year-old woman he once knew no longer existed. Unashamed and ripe for the taking, her seductive prose teased. Like quicksand under his feet, Matthew sank into the bliss of her nakedness that stood before him. He had never witnessed anything as beautiful as Jane's body. He lowered his head, encircled his lips around her nipple, and lost himself in the bulging comfort of her bosom.

Chapter 15

⁓ The Pleasures of the Flesh ⁓

Thankful that the few tense moments of the evening had passed, Jane relaxed as Matthew started a slow process of seduction. He didn't need to tempt her as she enthusiastically awaited the moment to enjoy his body. Since she had been with her fair share of male physiques, nothing compared to Matthew's as he began to rid himself of clothes. She helped to remove his shirt, undo the buttons of his trousers, and laughed, attempting to tug off his tight leather boots. When she had freed him of every stitch of clothing, her brow rose in surprise over his ample male endowment.

When he had taken her before, it was a rather speedy and crude event on her back. A quick unbuttoning to release himself, the uplifting of her skirt and an instant entrance into her virtue was all it took to get her pregnant. She had not particularly enjoyed the event since it was her first. It hurt, taking away any pleasure she might enjoy. As she thought back upon it, Matthew's youth had exposed his own lack of skill and experience. He had known nothing of pleasing her, and she wanted to know what he had learned over the years.

After they had eyed each other with pleasure, he drew her flush to his body, pressing his bare erection against her pelvis. With one hand behind her head to pull her to his lips and the other placed on the rounding of her breast, they exchanged heated kisses. Jane used her tongue as proficiently as he used his, and he enjoyed her intrusion into his mouth as well.

Both Matthew's hands slid down her body until each palm rested upon her cheeks. He kneaded her flesh with his fingers, bringing one hand forward. If he wanted to fondle her, she would rather experience it lying down. She pulled away, reclined on the bed, and motioned for him to join her.

"Come here, Matthew, and touch me," she said, in an enticing invitation. One knee she brought up, the other leg she let lie flat, and she flashed her garden of delight. He lowered himself next to her, and she took his hand, pulling it toward her moist treasure. It did not take long for Matthew to encircle his mouth upon hers and slip his long fingers inside. She moaned at the onslaught of pleasure she had missed for so long and drank in his deep kisses, enjoying the sensations of being fondled.

The longer he stroked her, the higher the need for a release. He pulled his lips away and gazed down at her with a wicked glint in his eye.

"Would you like more?" he breathed. "Like this?"

Whatever he had done to her, it sent her soaring into the heavens. He filled her with such expert massaging that it threw her uterus into spasms of delight. She groaned and sank her nails into the covers. "You wicked, wicked man," she cried.

"You have no idea how wicked your new companion can be," he drawled. Jane opened her eyes, her brow wet with sweat, and he pushed her hair away from her forehead. "Do you trust me?"

"Trust you for what?"

"I promise to pull out before release, but I must feel you inside, Jane. I must have you without anything between our flesh."

Jane did not like the method, as there were times men did not always retreat in time. As she thought about it, Matthew began stroking her again, resurrecting her pleasure spot until she writhed for more. The man was a devil in bed. "All right," she breathed nervously. "I trust you."

He removed his hand and put his knee between her legs, teasingly spreading her apart. When he had done so, he lowered himself and in one quick thrust sent her into a whimper of delight. Jane wrapped her legs around him. Matthew kissed and moved with such precision she moaned in satisfaction. As his tongue pushed inside her mouth and his hard, long shaft lunged deeper into her body, she found a level of enjoyment not yet experienced with any other.

When Matthew started to groan as if he could hold it no longer, a surge of panic flooded Jane's body. Nevertheless, as he promised, he pulled out and spilled his seed on her naked belly, bellowing his own release as he did.

"God, woman, you're enough to drive a man to madness," he gasped, rolling over on his back next to her. Jane took the corner of the sheet and wiped the evidence of his satisfaction off. He had come so swiftly that she surmised it had been some time since he lay with a woman.

"You have learned a few new tricks of your own," she remarked. "I daresay, Colonel, you know how to satisfy the ladies." Jane snickered at her top ten list, for if this were a foretaste of his skills, the man would remain her number one pick. His high standing, though, could become problematic comparing others in the future.

Matthew rolled on his side, propped his head up with his hand and elbow, and grinned at her with delight. He allowed his free hand to reach over to her breasts and play with the tip of her nipple.

"You are very capable in the pleasures of the flesh." He sighed. "You don't appear to have any inhibitions."

Jane's eyes sparkled. "There are many things I can do to bring you pleasure, Matthew. I'm also versed in some French ways of doing things."

"You don't say," he drawled, looking at her plump lips.

"I also enjoy various positions, especially when a man rolls me over and decides to ride me for pleasure."

"Good Lord, woman, have you no shame?" Matthew chortled.

"None whatsoever." She reached out and placed the palm of her hand on his chest, enjoying his taut, muscular form. "Your body is very pleasing," she remarked.

"As is yours," he replied. "For the most part, I'm finding this companionship arrangement quite satisfactory."

"Don't get too comfortable," Jane warned.

"I plan to get very comfortable," Matthew replied. "By the time I'm through with you, you may find every male after me a big bore."

Jane squirmed as he lightly pinched her nipple. "You rogue," she said, narrowing her eyes at him.

They lay side by side, speechless for a few minutes. Matthew's hands explored her breasts, and she ran her hands over his chest and arms. She never remembered him being so muscular, but perhaps his military service had toned his body to perfection.

Matthew started kissing her again. His hand released her breast and teasingly made its way down her body, following the curves and dips of her waist and hips. When he arrived at his destination, he threw his leg over hers and pushed her apart with his knee. Pinning her helplessly underneath, he watched for a few seconds as his fingers began exploring her vagina, arousing her once more. As she started to respond, he kissed her. Jane tried to articulate her thoughts.

"What are . . . "

He covered her mouth and silenced her for a few moments.

"What are you doing to me?" she gasped.

Matthew hushed her voice, expertly handling her, shoving her legs apart slightly more. He released her mouth, and she begged him.

"Please . . . "

"Please what?"

For the next few minutes, he teased her relentlessly, bringing her near the peak and halting. He held her captive in the bed, enjoying when she begged for more. Like a scoundrel enjoying his power, he would withdraw for a moment and ask, "More what?"

Engorged, swollen, and beseeching for satisfaction, she thought herself on the verge of madness. After one more plea and an expert maneuver with his fingers, her body shuddered in a violent orgasm. She groaned far too loud until it subsided, leaving her entire abdomen in a satisfied ecstasy. No man had ever made her enjoy it twice in one evening. After their first joining, Matthew had turned her into an addict. Jane opened her eyes to see him gazing down up her with a grin of victory.

"Enjoy that, did you?"

She brought the back of her hand to her forehead. "I'm beginning to think I've made a terrible mistake," she breathed in a whisper.

"No, Jane, you've made the right decision." Matthew withdrew his hand and pulled the covers over her naked body. He lay next to her, and Jane knew he stared at her in delight.

"Do you usually fall asleep afterward?"

"Sometimes," she admitted. "I think tonight may be one of them."

"I suppose you don't cuddle." He snickered.

"Not usually, though Neville liked to cuddle. The man is a big baby."

"Ah, yes, Neville. I need to remind myself this bed has entertained many men before me," he sighed. "I'm attempting to deal with the fact I'm no longer your one and only."

Matthew lay on his back silently for some time. Jane surmised that he must be wondering how many had gone before him. She held no inclination to tell him either but had an odd sense of shame touch her that it had perhaps been far too many. Had she not been careful in choosing her partners, she could have picked up more than lovers. Between avoiding pregnancy and embarrassing diseases, she had somehow kept herself safe. All those possibilities still existed, though, and she was no fool. Tempting fate could have its consequences.

For now, a sense of security enveloped her.

By her side lay a man who possessed the ability to satisfy her beyond her wildest imaginations. It would take some time to grow tired of his companionship unless they starting fighting or he did the unforgivable—declared his love.

"Do you mind if I lay my head on your shoulder?" she asked, scooting next to him.

He put his arm around her and drew her near. Jane found a comfortable spot and snuggled into it, hoping that it would alleviate Matthew of any pondering about her past partners.

"I have never been known to snore," she informed him.

"I wish I could say the same," Matthew admitted.

Jane draped her arm around his midsection, closed her eyes, and peacefully fell asleep.

CHAPTER 16
The Topic of Gossip

Within a week, Jane had received a frantic summons to her aunt's home to discuss an urgent matter. She worried that perhaps she had fallen ill or some other dire occurrence needed her involvement. When she arrived, Millicent accosted her at the door, dragged her into the parlor.

"What is the meaning of this?" Millicent ranted, shaking the newspaper in her face. "Have you read the gossip column? You're the talk of the ton."

"I occasionally do make the gossip headlines. What has piqued their interest this time?"

Millicent shoved the paper at her, pointing to the column. "Here, read it aloud. I think I shall faint," she said, fanning herself and sitting down on the settee.

Jane obeyed:

"*It has been reported that the scandalous Lady Jane has a new companion, none other than Colonel Rutland. The writer finds it quite surprising that a decorated war hero and widower, no less, has landed in the clutches of the ruthless female who leaves broken hearts strewn across the London landscape like discarded refuse. Surely, he deserves better because of his upstanding service to the country. Has anyone bothered to warn him of the dangers of such a dalliance? It would be a sad day indeed if the poor man died in battle, attempting to capture the cold and merciless heart of Jane Cavanagh."*

Usually, she would have giggled over the column. Today, however, she sat down next to her aunt, clutching the newspaper in her hand. "Oh dear," Jane moaned. "My reputation is becoming a bit wicked."

"Wicked, indeed! Why didn't you tell me that you have entered into a relationship with Colonel Rutland?" She reached over and squeezed Jane's hand until she crushed her fingers. "Jane, do you know what you're doing?"

She jerked her hand away from her aunt's clutches. "Yes, I know what I'm doing, and so does Matthew," she firmly replied. "We are both adults."

"Obviously, but does he know of your infamy for breaking hearts?"

"Oh, he knows, and he's been warned." Jane folded the paper and set it on the tea table in front of her.

"I have been in such a tizzy since I read the column I haven't been able to eat or sleep."

Millicent sighed, bringing the back of her hand to her forehead to add to the dramatics.

Jane patted her aunt's forearm. "Auntie, there is nothing to worry about. We are merely . . . " She halted her confession. "Well, you know."

"Already? You mean to say you've bedded him already?" Her eyes widened in astonishment.

"Yes," Jane smirked. "And it was a surprisingly pleasurable experience." She closed her eyes, recalling how satisfying it had been.

"Has he confessed his love to you?"

The question destroyed her musings, and Jane's eyelids shot open. "No, and I emphatically told him no babies, love, or marriage. He understands the rules."

Millicent shook her head. "For the life of me, I don't understand the power you wield over these men, Jane. It is astounding, frankly. No wonder half the women in London are jealous of your comings and goings."

"They should be jealous of my comings, indeed," she giggled. "Especially at the skillful hands of the colonel."

"Really," Millicent drawled. "Number one?"

"Oh yes, decidedly number one."

"I cannot believe I've lived my entire life and never known pleasure. Your uncle, God rest his soul, had no idea what to do. He rutted like a bull, and that was the end of it."

"I'm sorry, Auntie."

"Do tell, what is it like?"

Surprised at the question, Jane pondered a moment. "I don't think there are words in my vocabulary to describe the ecstasy when it happens. It's a mystery to me, but a wonderful mystery." A smile curled her lips. "It's like staring up at a mountain. You slowly climb and climb until you are nearly exhausted, attempting to reach the top. Then suddenly, you're at the peak, and when you arrive, you jump off and glide down into a serene green valley like a bird. It's a delightful experience."

"Hmmm. I have trouble imagining jumping off a mountaintop without being afraid for my life."

"When your heart beats furiously in your chest as you're climbing, you do fear for your life," Jane shuddered in a breath. "Matthew is an ardent lover."

"Don't you mean partner, dear?"

"Yes, yes, of course," she corrected herself, shrugging off her poor choice of words. "I hope Matthew doesn't see this, but as far as I know, he is not prone to reading the gossip column every morning."

"Don't you worry this might ruin his reputation, being publicly involved with you? Tongues will wag, that's for sure, when you are seen in public."

"It's nothing I can't deal with," Jane assured her. "He will probably shrug it off as I will."

"Does Neville know?"

"Yes. In fact, he warned Matthew of my ways, so you see, he knows what he's getting himself into."

"But why have you accepted him back into your life after what he did to you? You were so distressed when he returned."

"He seems to think that he owes me restitution of some sort for what happened between us," Jane explained. Her brow furrowed as she attempted to make sense of it herself. "He tells me he merely wants to be my companion, like the other men, but I don't believe him. Perhaps his conscience has caught up with him, and I'm not sure how to handle it."

"Interesting," she mused.

"Do you think it had anything to do with your conversation with him?" Jane inquired. "Even Neville seems to have the same opinion that he holds some responsibility for my so-called wayward life choices."

"I cannot conjecture about his motives," Millicent replied. "Nor can I guess about your own." She pondered for a moment about the situation and then added. "I worry, Jane, that he will fall in love with you. Will you push him aside as you've done all the others?"

"I have not thought that far ahead and am taking each day on its own merits. All I know is that I have much to learn about Matthew and am curious about the man he has become. No doubt, he is curious about me."

Gossip has a life of its own. It does not matter how hard you attempt to suppress it because it arrives in the most unwelcome places. As a rule, Lord Cavanagh ignored society's wagging tongues. However, when it came to reading about his daughter's escapades, they were entirely another matter. As he read the latest column, it incited him to rage. With the newspaper tucked under his arm and after a rather quick carriage ride to Rutland Park, he struck the knocker on the door with severity and anger.

"Where is he?" he bellowed as the butler opened the barrier.

"Who?" The servant jolted wide-eyed at the demand.

"Well, both! Sir Charles and Colonel Rutland, I demand an audience immediately."

"May I say who is calling?"

"Lord Cavanagh, you fool!" He pushed passed the butler, storming into the foyer.

"Please wait, and I'll announce your arrival."

"You do just that," he spat out in anger.

The butler disappeared down the hall and returned a few minutes later.

"They are currently eating breakfast but will receive you in the dining room."

"Good. Lead the way." Not waiting for an introduction, Lord Cavanagh burst into the room, waving the paper in the air like a madman.

"What is the meaning of this?" His voice demanded an answer.

Matthew and his father arched a glance at one another and then rose to their feet.

"I'm not sure what you are referring to, Lord Cavanagh." Sir Charles pointed to an empty chair. "Please, have a seat. Would you like a cup of tea?"

"I don't want a cup of tea," he snidely remarked. "I want answers."

"Well, perhaps I can give you one," Matthew said. "Might I read what has upset you, your lordship?"

"Here." Lord Cavanagh shoved the paper in his direction, pointing at the column. "I want to know the meaning of this."

As Matthew read the print, he stifled an amused grin. Apparently, he and Jane had made the gossip column. Matthew had not told his father about their reunion nor Jane's reputation and did not intend to do so now. He folded the paper and gave it back to Lord Cavanagh.

"It is just that, gossip. Jane and I are merely becoming reacquainted after the long years apart," he said, keeping his voice calm and even. "Nothing more."

"Rubbish," Lord Cavanagh replied. "I have it on good authority from my sister that you two are having an affair."

"An affair?" Sir Charles squawked, spinning his head toward his son. "Is that true, Matthew?" His brow furrowed in concern.

Instead of answering his father straightaway, Matthew narrowed his eyes at Lord Cavanagh.

"You don't seem to care very much about protecting your daughter's reputation by making such accusations when she is not here to defend herself."

"I'm fully aware of my daughter's reputation," Cavanagh barked. "There's no need to attempt to deceive me where she is concerned, young man."

"What reputation?" Sir Charles innocently asked.

Upset that Jane's character had been compromised in his father's eyes, Matthew endeavored to control the situation.

"Lord Cavanagh, do you mind if we take this conversation behind closed doors between the two of us?" He glanced at the confused face of his father. "I will speak to you afterward in private, sir."

"Very well. Do as you see fit," Sir Charles replied, sitting back down.

Matthew led his lordship into the parlor and then closed the door. Not taking a seat, he halted in front of him and expressed his concerns.

"I don't wish my father to know of your daughter's true reputation," he began. "That matter is not to be spoken of in front of him because he holds her in high esteem."

"I find it odd that you wish to protect her at all," he replied with a sour expression. "Nevertheless, I will agree." Lord Cavanagh pursed his lips.

"Be straight with me, Colonel, is this column true?" He held the paper up to his face, sounding slightly calmer than he did a moment ago.

"We have agreed to reacquaint ourselves with one another," Matthew replied in a noncommittal tone.

"Am I to assume that means in a sexual nature as well?"

"That is something you'll need to discuss with Jane, I'm afraid. A gentleman does not divulge what he does with a lady behind closed doors."

"She's no lady, and you of all people should know that," he growled. "If it weren't for you, she would be quite different from the woman she has become."

Peeved at the accusation, Matthew shot back. "I never thought you held enough regard for Jane to care what type of woman she was," he snidely remarked.

Instead of admitting anything, his lordship turned his wrath on Matthew. "It's your damn fault," he bellowed. "You were the one who seduced her, got her pregnant, and then discarded her like rubbish." His face turned beet red as he continued to shake the gossip column Matthew's face. "Frankly, I'm appalled that my daughter has even allowed you back into her life."

"Jane and I have come to an agreement. That is all you need to know," Matthew reiterated.

"So help me God, if you break her heart

again, there'll be hell to pay," he threatened in a deep voice, pointing his index finger. "And you damn well better not get her pregnant again!" He spun around and opened the door. "Heed my warning, Colonel Rutland," he roared. "Or I shall put a bullet in your skull." His lordship exited Rutland Park in haste, slamming the door behind him.

Matthew thrust his hand through his hair, astonished at the fury Lord Cavanagh had exhibited. How in the world did that bit of gossip land in the hands of the newspapers? He had only been with her one time, and they had not even attended a social function together as a couple. As he stood, ruminating with a scowl over the situation, his father entered the room.

"Oh dear," Sir Charles said. "It doesn't appear Lord Cavanagh is too happy about you courting his daughter," he innocently remarked.

"No, he doesn't appear to be," Matthew agreed. "But we are not courting, Father. Merely spending time with one another to renew old acquaintances." He hated lying, but his father always liked Jane, and he could not bear him knowing the truth of her way of life.

"Well, no objections on my part, son." He patted Matthew's upper arm. "Come, let's finish breakfast before it gets cold."

Matthew decided that he and Jane needed to speak of the matter as he did not care to be the center of society's attention.

Chapter 17

⟨ Much Ado About Everything ⟩

Matthew had already planned to meet Jane at her town house that evening for pleasure and intended to speak about the hullabaloo in the gossip column. When he arrived at her door and she opened it, Jane shook the paper in front of him.

"We have made the news," she chortled with a gleeful look in her eyes.

"I've heard," he said, surprised that she was amused when he had considered it appalling. He closed the door and grabbed the paper out of her hands. "Dear Lord, you've even circled it with ink," he remarked. "Do you cut these out and save them like trophies?" He hoped to God he was not about to become the next in a long line of scandalous gossip column references tucked away in some keepsake box.

"No," she quickly answered, "but now that you mention it, such a collection would make nice mementos. I'll keep that in mind."

"Amusing," he remarked, feeling no enjoyment at the thought of having his scandals kept on file.

"Does it bother you?" she asked, flopping on the settee, fanning herself with the folded newspaper.

"I don't care to be the subject of gossip for others to discuss behind my back," he remarked with sincerity. "There doesn't seem much can be done about it, but for the life of me how did they get that tidbit of news so quickly? We haven't even been seen together at a public function to cause chin-wagging."

"I wondered that myself," Jane admitted. "Perhaps one of our acquaintances with ulterior motives, like Neville."

"I hardly think Neville is that vindictive," he said, dismissing the idea. "What about Lord Grisham?"

"Possible," Jane mused.

Irritated at the subject, Matthew took a moment to gaze upon her attire. She wore an ivory-colored dress trimmed in lace with an embroidered blue flower pattern along the hemline. The choice of color made her appear innocent as an angel, but she was a devil in disguise.

"Wearing undergarments this evening?" he asked, eyeing her bosom as he hovered above her.

"As a matter of fact, I thought that I would make you work for your taste of honey tonight," she teased.

"Not before we talk about the column," he

said, taking the newspaper from her hand and setting it down on the table.

"What is there to talk about?" she balked.

"Well, this morning your father arrived at Rutland Park, waving the paper in my face."

Immediately, Jane grabbed Matthew's hand and pulled him down next to her on the seat. "You don't say?" she remarked, her mouth gaping open.

"Frankly, it surprised the hell out of me," he began somberly. "He came during breakfast and started ranting at me in front of my father. I pulled him aside to the parlor to have a word with him privately."

"Why? Doesn't your father know about us?" Jane asked.

"I have attempted to safeguard your reputation in his eyes, Jane. He is fond of you, you know."

"How chivalrous to protect my character," she replied with an air of irritation. "You should be honest with him."

"He is my father, and I shall tell him what I wish him to know," Matthew asserted.

"And what is that?"

"I've explained to him that we are becoming reacquainted with one another."

"I see," she pondered. "And what did my father have to say about the matter?"

"Much, I'm afraid." Matthew pulled his eyes away and glanced at the decanter of alcohol on a table across the room. "Do you mind if I have a drink?"

"Well, if you need a drink to tell me what my father had to say, help yourself. You might as well pour me one too because I'm flabbergasted that he had anything to say at all."

Matthew rose to his feet. He sniffed the contents of the decanter and detected brandy. Pouring two glasses, he returned and handed one to Jane, then sat down by her side. After taking a sip, he continued.

"Well, let's see if I can recall the entire gist of his raving comments," he began. "First, he accused us of having an affair, but I put off his comment by saying we were merely getting reacquainted. He didn't believe me, so I told him to ask you if he wanted the truth."

"Oh, wonderful." Jane heaved an exasperated sigh. "I suppose this means he will be dropping by any day now to give me a piece of his mind. What else?"

"I've been warned to not break your heart or to get you pregnant," Matthew announced with a sly grin.

"Well, I hope you assured him that you would not be doing either of those things," she said sternly as if to remind him again.

"Not in so many words," Matthew admitted. "In fact, I don't think I promised I wouldn't do any of those things."

Jane had been sipping her brandy, and his

remarked caused her to choke. After coughing to regain a breath of air, her eyes widened. "You damn well better not get me pregnant." Her face reddened as she threatened him.

"But it's all right if I break your heart?" he jested with a lopsided smile.

"I have no heart to break, Matthew. When will you accept that reality?" She pulled her eyes away from him, staring across the room to avoid the discussion.

Matthew did not answer because he knew her words were merely a ruse. Underneath her hardened shell lay a heart that he intended to find again. He was not quite sure how, but until he discovered where it was hidden, he would not relent in his battle to expose it.

"If you insist, Jane, but that doesn't solve the problem with the gossip business. Doesn't it bother you, or don't you care?" Matthew asked in a vexed tone.

She shrugged her shoulders. "Not really. Worse things have been said about me, so I give it no heed. If the writer is attempting to taint my already scandalous reputation, what harm can she or he do? As for you, well, you may receive letters from a few of my past acquaintances with firm warnings to escape alive while you can." She giggled a wicked laugh and then drank the remainder of her glass.

"I'm bored," she announced, pulling her skirt up and showing her upper thigh. "Aren't you interested in discovering what I'm wearing under my dress?"

"Eventually," he said, ignoring her teasing seduction. "I would like to talk."

"Talk? About what?"

Matthew reached over and tugged her hem down. "Oh, I don't know," he mused aloud. "Just idle chitchat." He sipped his drink, savoring it bit by bit. "So, do you have any interests?"

"Interests?" She scrunched her nose in aversion.

"You know, reading, the theater, needlepoint, horseback riding, archery—those types of things."

Jane gawked at him and then shook her head. "I wouldn't mind riding this evening," she replied, inching her skirt up again. Jane battled her eyelashes like a prostitute, trying to lure him to bed. He wondered if she ever thought of anything else.

"I'll consider the position," he replied nonchalantly, "if you answer my question."

"Oh, for goodness' sake," she complained. "I don't care about much of anything." She let out a puff of air from her lungs.

"You mean all you care about is sensuality?"

"Well, not all the time," she said, lowering her eyes as if she were embarrassed to admit that was the totality of her personality.

"I remember that you enjoyed poetry. Do you still indulge when you have the time?"

Matthew glanced around the room and noticed a small bookcase. He rose to his feet and walked over to the collection, reading the titles. A book by Lord Byron caught his eye. "By the condition of the book, it appears you've read it quite a bit."

"And what if I have?" Jane defended herself.

"Do you have any favorites you would like to read me?" Matthew returned with the book in hand and gave it to Jane. She hesitated to take it but eventually relented. A slight blush pinked her cheeks.

"You're embarrassing me," she admitted in a low tone.

"Why? Because I want to know more about you than what is hidden under your skirt? I'm sure you are a fascinating woman beyond the bedchamber, Jane." He took the book from her hand and set it down on the table. "If you're uncomfortable, then perhaps another time."

"And what are your interests?" She turned the tables on him quickly, taking the focus from herself.

"I haven't had time, being in the military, to focus on much of anything," he admitted. "It wasn't until I married Felicity and she became with child that I found interest in something beyond my profession." Resurrecting the past pulled him into a contemplative mood.

"How did you meet?" Jane's voice was tender and inquisitive.

"I came home on a three-month furlough to

see Father, and we met through friends of the family. It was a short courtship. It's not easy being married in the military, but I had already planned to sell my commission upon my tenth year of service."

"I'm surprised, as I had been under the impression that you wished to maintain a career."

"After the war, I had had enough," Matthew confessed. "Then Felicity became pregnant, came to term, and died bearing our stillborn son." He gulped the remaining drink and set down the glass. "You know I had hoped to talk about you, Jane, and not my past. Somewhere I lost control of the conversation," he smirked, wanting to change the subject.

"I apologize for prying. No more talk of the past. I'd rather focus on the present," she reticently admitted.

Jane pulled her skirt again, and Matthew eyed her thigh. He slipped the palm of his hand on her leg and slowly let it glide upward. Her soft skin felt glorious to the touch, and he teasingly crept his way upward until he touched linen fabric.

"Well, this is an obstruction that needs removal," he announced. "I think we need to retire to your bedchamber, Lady Jane, so I can determine what needs to be done."

He rose to his feet and held out his hand, which Jane took. Instead of walking together, he scooped her up in his arms and carried her up the stairs. The room awaited him with lit candles, incense, and the coverlets of her bed already pulled back, revealing the pristine white sheets. After sitting her down on the edge of the bed, he knelt on one knee and took off her shoes, one by one.

"Very nice silk stockings," he complimented her while gently pulling them down each leg. Matthew made no effort to care for her garments as he threw each of them to the side on the floor. "What is under that dress?" he said, sticking his head underneath her skirt.

"You scoundrel," Jane screamed. "Get out from underneath there."

He ignored her plea and pushed aside the layer of chemise under her dress, revealing her bare bottom. Apparently, she did not care for the crotchless shorts that some women wore. The practice was fine for him, as it gave easy access.

Laughing at her continued banter to remove his head, he did so. He rose to his feet and pulled her upright. "Turn around, dearest, so I can undo the buttons to your dress." He swore that he sensed a slight tremble under Jane's skin and smiled at the thought that anticipation of what was to come had caused her to shudder.

Matthew removed her gown, her chemise, and enjoyed her naked form standing before him. His hands touched the roundness of her bottom as he pulled her toward him, kissing her deeply. Jane's suggestion of a specific position aroused him as he imaged bending her over and riding her with deep thrusts.

"I hunger for you, Jane. I could eat you alive," he breathed heavily, kissing her neck.

"Then eat," she drawled. "I wouldn't want you to starve, Colonel."

He gently turned her around and grinned wickedly. "Get in position," he commanded in a gruff tone as if he were giving orders to his men in the regiment. She smiled in response, apparently enjoying the demand. Jane bent face down on the bed, spreading her legs apart and leaving her derriere in the air for his eyes to enjoy. "Stay put while I remove these damn clothes. In the meantime, you can think about what's coming," he teased.

His words caused her to groan, and she wiggled her ass at him, waiting for his arrival. Jane's lack of inhibition shocked him. Nothing in the bedroom seemed to phase her one bit. She acted like a debased whore but was a delicious candy-covered cherry he could eat forever. What man wouldn't want to make her his wife? He would never stray with a woman like her to possess the rest of his days.

Finally undressed, he approached her from behind. He put his hands on her buttocks, handling the roundness and teasing her in anticipation. It would be a delightful evening of getting to know Jane on a deeper level.

Chapter 18
⁓ The Talk of the Ton ⁓

Only a few weeks remained of the season, and Jane and Matthew openly attended social functions as a couple, becoming the center of attention. People whispered, heads shook, eyes widened, and a few men pulled Matthew aside to talk sense into him. Matthew discarded their concerns, as he found the conversations intrusive into his private affairs.

On the other hand, the burden of who she had become lay heavily upon his conscience. Her shameful reputation nearly embarrassed him to be seen with her in public. To make matters worse, he was enjoying every inch of her shocking behavior behind closed doors with little remorse.

Neville on one occasion cornered him at a soiree during intermission, making his private inquiry into their affairs. Matthew's newfound busy schedule had prevented him from spending time with Neville, and frankly, their relationship had strained because of his involvement with Jane.

"You have drifted away into the arms of Jane,"

Neville whined. "If I don't mind saying, she appears to keep you quite busy." He snickered with a knowing glint in his eye.

"We actually do other things besides what you're referring to," Matthew somberly replied.

Neville's brow arched in surprise. "I find that somewhat hard to believe based on my previous relationship with the woman. She has little else on her mind."

"There is more to Jane than meets the bedsheets, and I intend to uncover that as well." Matthew threw a determined look at his friend. "I'm rediscovering the lady that I once knew in more than one way."

Neville studied him for a moment and then coyly grinned at Matthew. "Oh, I see your plot," he snidely remarked. "You are attempting another tactic to gain her affections. Giving the woman attention." He sighed. "I've been told that the way to a woman's heart is to show interest in her mundane affairs. Is that your tactic? If it is, good luck."

"Perhaps," Matthew replied. He shrugged his shoulders, not wishing to show commitment to any plan lest it lead to another lecture from Neville on the dangers of being with Jane.

"Are you enjoying the bedsheets?" Neville asked in a low tone.

Irritated at Neville's inquiry in public, Matthew narrowed his eyes in displeasure. "A gentleman never reveals to another gentleman what transpires behind closed doors," he tersely remarked. "I know we are friends, Neville, but give me a bit more credit than to dishonor Jane in a public setting while you listen."

"There's nothing left to dishonor," he replied in a tone of bitterness. "You forget that I shared those bedsheets long before you. I'm quite aware of what transpires on and underneath them."

Matthew sensed the animosity between them rising to an unwholesome level and curtly bowed. "If you'll excuse me," he announced. "I need to return to Lady Jane."

The evening affair had turned into a somewhat uncomfortable event. Matthew wondered if this would be his lot as her companion for months on end. Thankfully, the season would soon be over, and the tongue-wagging crowds would return to their country homes. Perhaps the two of them would be able to find some semblance of peace afterward. He decided to speak with Jane about leaving London for a trip. Bath or Brighton might give them a reprieve and time to focus upon each other in more ways than one singular purpose.

He returned to his seat and discovered Jane by herself, appearing a bit forlorn in her countenance. "Is everything all right?"

She brought her fan to her face and discreetly spoke to him behind it.

"Do you mind if we leave early, Matthew?" She brandished a pitiful gaze. "I am afraid that I have a dreadful headache."

"Yes, of course." The musicians had just begun the next selection, and Matthew rose to his feet. Jane followed, and he escorted her out of the room. A few heads turned in their direction, but Matthew ignored their stares. As they exited and found themselves outdoors in the fresh air, Jane heaved a sigh of relief.

"A bit stuffy indoors, don't you think?" Her eyes glanced up, and he took her meaning.

"Yes, I discovered the same," he said with a tone of sadness. Matthew took Jane's hand in his and gave it a sweet kiss. "Headache better?"

"Much," she mischievously grinned. "In fact, it's disappeared."

"What would you like to do?" he asked.

"We are only a mile from my town house. Why don't we take a leisurely stroll home?" Jane suggested.

The comfortable evening temperature, the almost-full moon, and the few stars visible above were all the incentive that Matthew needed to agree. He offered her arm, and Jane took it, tugging him close to her side. He began a leisurely walking pace, feeling far better than he had a half hour ago.

"Is it always this way?" Matthew asked.

"What way?"

"The looks, whispers, and overt comments at the social gatherings which you attend with a companion." Matthew found it tiresome.

"Not usually, but it appears that you have brought me more attention than even I care to receive," Jane admitted. "For the most part, I don't experience shunning or ill-at-ease glances. When with Neville, society seemed to think us a gregarious pair, and we were welcomed with opened arms."

"Why the change with me on your arm?" Matthew scowled.

Jane halted for a moment and looked at him with an out-of-character glint of approval in her eyes. "Because, Matthew, you are well respected as a war hero. Your name and reputation have no tarnish upon them whatsoever. By associating yourself with me, society believes that I am harming you, and they don't approve."

"Or they don't approve of my decision to be with you," he added with certainty. Matthew resumed their steps as he pondered Jane's explanation. "I find that fascinating and infuriating all in the same breath."

"I'm afraid this week has not gone well for me either," Jane admitted. "My father paid me a visit yesterday."

"Why didn't you say something earlier?" Matthew asked with a questioning glance.

"I hoped to keep you from concern," Jane answered. "But no bother. I set him straight regarding the matter."

"The last thing I want to do, Jane, is to come between you and your father," Matthew admitted with concern. Jane burst out laughing.

"There is nothing to come between us. Do not worry about our relationship. The man puffs like a pillow in anger, but when you punch back with a few words, there is no substance and he quickly deflates."

They walked a few more blocks, and Jane tugged on his arm a few times, making sure they were close side by side. Eventually, she asked what the others had to say to him that evening.

"Did you receive any advice to run away while you still can?"

"Oh yes, a few remarks. However, I'm disappointed to say that Neville and I are still not seeing eye to eye." He sighed in resignation.

Jane halted again. "Oh dear. Am I the cause of it? I don't wish our companionship to ruin your friendship with him."

"I cannot say that it has, but I sense an underlying bitterness that lingers regarding your treatment of him." Matthew brought his hand to her cheek and brushed it slightly with his fingertips. "You look quite lovely in the moonlight." He winked, wanting to change the subject. Gossips, Neville, and her father had all intruded upon their private moments, and he wished to push them out of mind.

"Flattery? Usually, men wield it like a weapon to an unsuspecting woman, but I know exactly what your intentions are, Colonel."

"Do you, Lady Jane?"

He wondered if she had begun to understand his motivations that went far beyond the bedroom. Regardless, he found Jane a fascinating woman who had hidden the gems of her personality behind a facade of scandalous behavior. Somewhere in the years that they had been apart she had lost the essence of the woman she could have become. A loving wife and a wonderful mother. In his bid for her emotions, he wanted Jane to realize her worth beyond the skills she possessed in her bedchamber. She was a treasure, indeed, in so many ways.

"Now that the season is coming to a close, would you have any objection to taking a trip together?"

"What kind of trip?" she asked.

"Anywhere where we are not known and can enjoy each other on our own terms," he suggested. "Bath perhaps? Brighton?"

Jane burst out in laughter. "Oh, my dear Matthew. You have no idea how far my influence has spread across the landscape."

"Apparently not," he replied with an arched brow. "Do tell?"

"Well, Bath is out of the question as quite a few of my social acquaintances, including my aunt and father, will no doubt be there in the next few weeks to take up residence."

"Well, that will not do," he said with disappointment. "And what of Brighton?"

"Others I know will be there too, so I prefer

not to visit."

"I suppose we could just remain in London if everyone is going elsewhere," he replied, not caring for the idea one bit. "Would you consider a trip up north, perhaps to Scotland?"

She glanced at him and seriously asked, "Only if you promise to wear a kilt."

"A kilt." He laughed. "Not my choice of garment, but if the lady insists, I might be able to accommodate the request."

Jane squeezed his arm, and her face glowed with an air of excitement. "I have never been to Scotland," she admitted. "It will be a dreadfully long trip, though, won't it?"

"Ten days by coach," Matthew admitted. "Perhaps longer."

"Awful," Jane replied, scrunching her nose at the thought of the inconvenience. "I would rather not spend that much time captive inside a rocking carriage just to see your naked manhood underneath a kilt."

As they neared Jane's town house, Matthew had exhausted all ideas. Society conveniently strangled their options to escape and find time for themselves away from peeping eyes and gossip. Had they been husband and wife, it would be a much different scenario. There would be no scandal and nothing of interest unless affairs regrettably resulted by either one straying to another's bed. The thought deeply troubled Matthew, and by the time they reached the stoop and entered the foyer of her residence, he found himself in the doldrums.

"I don't know how you have survived being the center of attention," he acknowledged. "I must admit that I'm finding the overt exposure unwelcome."

"It will pass as time does. The notoriety of the two of us being together will die down and by next season be all but forgotten."

Jane placed the palm of her hand on the side of his face, which he found oddly comforting but incongruous on her part.

"Well, if you would rather not escape the city, we can watch the ton dissipate and enjoy London on our own. Perhaps you wouldn't mind an occasional trip to Rutland Park to visit my father."

"Perhaps," she said, taking his hand. She gently led him upstairs to her bedchamber. "I really need something far more than a trip to Scotland. Do you mind if we travel a short distance to my bed instead?"

Of course he did not mind. He hungered for her often, an endless, aching need. The thought of her pushing him away should he express his love or desire for something more kept his lips silent. Inside his chest, however, his heart swelled with a growing love for Jane that he feared would burst from between his lips only to fall upon deaf ears.

Jane, on the other hand, had displayed no amorous affection toward him that would betray her sentiments. The only emotions expressed were merely sexual in nature as she groaned through each pleasurable climax. Even though she had convinced herself she had no heart, Matthew was determined to prove her wrong.

Chapter 19
ᗅ An Unwelcome Emotion ᗅ

It did not take long for Matthew to undress Jane and tenderly lay her upon the bed. She closed her eyes, not wanting to see his. They often burned with want and need, but at times she noted something more in his soul. It was like a curtain that opened for a second, revealing an unwelcome flash of love. When he feared exposure, Matthew shut his eyes and buried his head in her neck. Afterward, he would kiss her excessively and become more sexually aggressive in nature.

Obviously, Jane welcomed his advances. The man was by far the best erotic partner she had enjoyed. Not once did he fail to bring her to a peak of pleasure, often before he satisfied himself. When she found herself jumping off the mountaintop to glide down in utter bliss, he would thrust inside her until he too took the journey, grunting as men often do upon release.

As she lay in his arms afterward, he stroked her gently. At times they would talk, and at others they would drift peacefully off to sleep. Jane felt secure in his embrace, a sensation she had not experienced with other men in her bed. Matthew gave her more attention, showing his interest in her beyond what they shared sexually. If she did not know any better, he was attempting to provide her with a taste of matrimonial bliss, if that existed.

Her mind wandered to troublesome thoughts that his affections would soon ruin their companionship. The idea of losing him bothered her deeply. It was time to remind him that she only wanted to use his body and had no interest in his heart. Jane climbed on top of Matthew and straddled his torso, taking his shaft into her hands.

"Am I not to rest this evening?" he asked with a raised brow, watching her skillfully excite him to perform.

"I'm feeling empty," she pouted. "I don't like being empty."

When she had successfully aroused him again, Jane took the lead. She lowered herself and slowly filled her emptiness. Enjoying the sensation of being gratified by his body, Jane tilted her head back and moaned from the splendid pleasure of his ample flesh. Matthew reached out with both hands and clutched her breasts, kneading them and playing with her nipples.

"Lay still," she ordered. "Let me do the work."

"This could be dangerous," he warned. "Are

you throwing restraint to the wind?" he asked.

Overcome by the pleasure, her wanton desires dominated her focus. Matthew said something, but her brain ignored the words. With closed eyes, she failed to see Matthew's concerned frown. All she heard was his moans of pleasures as she took from him what she wanted, thrusting herself up and down upon his body in a frenzy to climb the peak.

"Jane," he warned. "Jane, stop, or I'll spill my seed in you!"

As he cautioned her, she groaned her own climax, and suddenly Matthew grabbed her and pushed her off, throwing her on top of the mattress. The shocking move in his part caught her by surprise, and she landed on the bed next to him with a thud.

"Why did you do that?" she whined, coming to less than an exciting end. Rather than gliding into the valley, she crashed headlong.

"Are you trying to get pregnant?" he shouted in anger, sitting up, and glaring at her.

His accusation startled her. "Oh my God, I'm sorry," she confessed, bringing her hand to her mouth. Still panting from the physical exertion, she sputtered, "I didn't—I didn't think." Jane's pleasure swiftly drained away. Matthew had agreed to be careful and had continued to be each time they joined. She had committed a foolish act that startled her to an unwanted realization. As Jane thought about what had transpired and her recklessness, her heart sank into an abyss of despair. She glanced up at him and spoke in calm realization.

"I've become too comfortable with you," she admitted. Her brow furrowed over the disturbing thought that she had come dangerously close to making a terrible mistake.

"What's that supposed to mean?" Matthew asked, scowling at her. "Haven't I kept my part? No babies—no love—and God knows, no marriage." His voice grated with deep hurt.

"And you have," she admitted, looking at his distraught countenance. "I don't like being comfortable with any man, Matthew, or I cannot guard my heart."

Slow-burning anger radiated from his eyes. In a terse voice, he spoke. "You are so intent on not falling in love that you make a mockery of every man you join yourself with in bed."

Matthew swung his feet over the edge of the mattress and sat up. He shoved both hands through his unruly hair, displaying his frustration. Had it been any other male sitting there, her heart would have remained unmoved by his actions. She had hurt him, and the atmosphere in the room turned heavy and suffocating. As she watched him breathe in and out with ragged breaths and lower his head in a painful display of emotions, she felt a nudge of empathy flow through her heart. The emotion had not shown life for anyone in years, but as Matthew sat there, she feared the worst had begun to happen. Something had to be done.

"Perhaps we should call it an evening, dearest," she announced. "I'm afraid we both have had a difficult few days, and it's putting a strain upon our arrangement."

"Agreed," Matthew huffed. "Let's not strain the arrangement," his bitter voice replied. He stood, grabbed his clothes from the chair, and began to dress. Jane could not bear to watch him, so she lay on the bed, turned in the opposite direction, and covered herself with the sheet. The beating of her heart against her rib cage increased to a frightening level as she feared the time had already arrived to start shoving him away. It had been far too short an arrangement, which saddened her. Eventually, she needed to break his heart because she could not bear giving hers to any man.

After he had fully dressed, she rolled over and glanced at him. He stood by the bed, staring at her with indecision on his face. With pursed lips and a tense jawline, Jane knew he too felt torn.

"Let us take a break for a few days," he suggested. "Between society and the inability to control ourselves sexually, I'm a bit exhausted."

"I understand," Jane replied, not arguing the point.

"It would be nice if you could come to dinner at Rutland Park next week," Matthew proposed.

"Father would enjoy seeing you."

"Yes, that would be pleasant," she agreed. "As long as we stay away from the maze, I shall act like a proper young lady for your father's sake."

"Fine. I'll speak with him," Matthew replied coolly. "I'll send word by a messenger of the date."

"Sounds wonderful," Jane replied, smiling at him.

He remained straight-faced. "Good night, Jane."

"Good night, Matthew."

With those words, he left her bedroom, trotted downstairs, and exited her residence, quietly closing the door. Their relationship had begun to unravel like a ball of twine. It frightened Jane because once untied, the result would be a tangled web of emotions that would never be healed.

Chapter 20
Unraveling Ties

As the weeks passed and the end of the season neared, Matthew saw an alteration in Jane. They continued their companionship and sexual encounters, but she raised a hedge around her heart that appeared higher than when they had first started consorting with one another. Also, Matthew's conscience soured with guilt. The more his love grew for her, the deeper his culpability burdened his soul. He didn't want her to be a sexual companion. He wanted to be her husband and give Jane the respect and love she desperately needed.

No matter how hard he tried to woo her beyond the superficiality of their relationship, she rejected his attempts. The hope he once held weakened, and his resolve grew weary. Perhaps he should have listened to everyone before embarking on a doomed campaign. He had caused her hardened heart, but the decisions she made afterward were her folly alone. Jane could not see her worth, and it placed a heavy sorrow on Matthew's heart that she would probably never transform into a respectable woman.

All the same, Matthew continued marching to the ultimate battlefield that would play out between them. He wondered how much longer Jane intended to keep him dangling on a leash like her favorite dog. As fate would have it, though, he received news that would bring their companionship to its own culmination very soon.

As Jane predicted, the ton's fascination with their affair waned, for which Matthew found great relief. They received an invitation to attend the last formal ball of the season. In attendance were the usual guests such as Lady Whitmore and her lady friends.

Neville arrived with a new love interest on his arm by the name of Charity Atwood, the daughter of a baron. She had taken an eye to him during the Westlake's affair during supper, and Neville had lately reciprocated her interest. Matthew excused himself from Jane for a moment to pull Neville aside and congratulate him on his latest triumph. Charity had stepped away momentarily.

"I've come to congratulate you," Matthew said, approaching. "She's a bit young, but a rare beauty indeed."

"Oh, so you have taken the time to notice," Neville replied. An air of irritation remained between them.

"Of course I noticed. Though we don't speak as often, I am still pleased to see you happy."

Neville softened his countenance. "She is a rare beauty as well as intelligent and kind. I daresay that I may ask her for her hand in marriage."

"I'm glad to hear of it," Matthew sincerely replied.

"And what of you?" Neville asked. "As much as I hate to tell you, you're nearing the timeline that Jane usually decides to move on."

"I'm sensing it as we speak," Matthew admitted. He dejectedly lowered his gaze to the floor.

"And your bid to win her heart?" Neville's tone was laced with empathy, knowing already the attempt had failed.

"The woman is an impenetrable fortress," Matthew said, forcing a strained grin. "But I am not ready to concede to defeat just yet."

Matthew noted Neville's eyes shift across the ballroom to where he had left Jane speaking with her aunt.

"As a friend, I would caution you again," Neville said, nodding in Jane's direction. "It appears the Duke of Wharton has caught her attention. Her fan is trifling with him."

Matthew's eyes quickly shifted over toward Jane. A tight knot formed in his gut as he observed her actions and the duke's blatant response to her flirtation.

"Matthew," Neville said, leaning discreetly toward his ear. "Rumor has it he's made her an offer. He wants Jane as his mistress." Neville paused, clearly distressed, by the look of his furrowing brow. He reached out and touched Matthew on his upper arm. "Be careful, my friend. Be very careful." He patted him and then dropped his hand.

As if a bayonet at the end of a rifle had pierced his chest, Matthew sensed a searing pain slice through his soul. An overwhelming sense of anguish sucked the breath from his lungs as he witnessed the duke's interest and Jane's reciprocation. At that moment, Matthew realized the bitter taste of defeat. He had to cease the futility of his quest to win Jane and decided to do so immediately.

"Thank you for the warning," Matthew replied in a hoarse voice.

"You were warned," Neville expressed in a compassionate tone. "The ton is filled with new and eager young virgins in quest of a husband. For God's sake, Matthew. Open your eyes and seek a bride elsewhere."

"That chance may never come," Matthew replied, returning his eyes to Neville. "I received word yesterday that I've been called back to active duty."

"What?"

"Ironic, isn't it? Perfect timing as fate would deal me."

"Does Jane know?"

"She's about to find out," Matthew replied. "Excuse me, Neville."

Eager to put an end to the uncomfortable scenario playing out before Matthew's eyes, he walked back toward Jane to rejoin her as she continued her coquettish discussion with the duke. When he came to her side, she quickly halted her antics and smiled at him. The duke, on the other hand, eyed him as if he were assessing his enemy.

"Your Grace," Matthew said, not waiting for an introduction from Jane.

"Colonel," he replied, as if he already knew everything about him.

"His Grace and I were just chatting about the fine weather we're having this season," Jane announced innocently.

Matthew's brow rose. "The weather?" he challenged her in front of the duke.

"Yes," the duke replied. "I have invited Lady Jane—and you, of course—to my estate for a weekend house party in June."

"June, you say?" Matthew's brow rose. He was not a man prone to making rash decisions, but at that moment, something inside him cracked.

"I'm afraid I shall not be able to attend," he replied somberly. "I have been called back to active duty. The British are forming with the Prussian army to stand against Napoleon."

Jane's gregarious countenance faded into dismay. "What do you mean, you have been called back to duty?"

The duke, apparently having the sense to

allow them to have a private conversation, quickly excused himself. No doubt at that moment he believed his bid for Jane had been fortuitously granted by Providence's intervention. With Matthew out of the picture, Jane would undoubtedly accept his offer.

"Please excuse me, but I believe this is a conversation that should continue without me. It appears the two of you need to speak."

He turned on his heel and left them standing alone. As he did so, Matthew could not bear to hear the words Jane would soon say to him. He had gone over whatever speech she would make a thousand times, bracing himself for the moment. Their time together would end, and he, like all the others, would be tossed aside in her pursuit for a new meaningless relationship.

"I meant to speak to you about this, Jane, as duty calls me back to the front," he began, giving her no time to object.

"Is this about Napoleon's escape from Elba?" she pressed.

"Yes. The British and Prussian armies are gathering forces, and my regiment will be leaving within the week. I was going to tell you this evening."

Matthew used the occurrence as an excuse rather than waiting. As he spoke of his intent, it all made sense. It would be a perfect way to part ways with Jane, sparing him the embarrassment of her discarding him. He would rather die on the battlefield than see her take up with the duke as his mistress. As he gazed into her eyes, the thought of losing her to another possessed the power to send him to his death before reaching the frontline.

"I don't understand why you need to return to service," Jane replied. "Surely the British Army can do without you."

"Jane, I did not resign my commission. I retired taking half pay, which allows the army to recall me to active duty when needed." He paused, seeing a pained expression take over her beautiful countenance. He dismissed her reaction as a momentary shock rather than any type of amorous affection for him. Matthew inhaled before speaking his last words.

"Besides, you can do without me, Jane. I'm merely a temporary placement. I knew that when this relationship began." He halted for a moment and picked her hand up in his and kissed it. "I can see the change in the weather as well as any other. I'm no fool, although I have been a fool for you," he admitted somberly. No longer needing to suppress his feelings for fear of losing her, he spoke them truthfully. "I love you beyond measure," his voice cracked. "Of that, I am sure. Nevertheless, I know that you hold no affection for me. So I release you, my love, to the next who has caught your eye. I'm sure the duke will enjoy your bed like all the rest."

Perhaps it had been a cruel place to say his

departing words, but Matthew could not bear being alone in a room with Jane, which would have prolonged the discussion to an agonizing length. The music and the dancing couples swirled around, unaware of what had transpired between them. All he knew was that this would be the last time he would be with Jane, perhaps forever. The bittersweet moment sent his heart thumping against his rib cage.

"Goodbye, Jane," he said, bending down and giving her a soft kiss on her cheek. "Be happy."

His lips lingered for a second, and Jane stood rigid. With great difficulty, he smiled at her warmly, turned, and walked away. Matthew passed her aunt, nodded, but said nothing. Tomorrow he would return to the regiment to fight another battle that he no doubt had a greater chance of winning than the one he had just retreated from in the form of Jane.

Jane watched Matthew walk away in an air of defeat. It was the second time in her life she had observed the military take him away. Shocked at his hasty departure, leaving her behind in a room crowded with attendees, her eyes scanned the scene. She caught the gaze of Neville, who apparently had been watching their interaction. He must have had something to do with Matthew's sudden change of mind, so she walked over to him, interrupting his conversation with Lady

Atwood.

"Do you mind if I have a private conversation with the viscount?" she asked. "I promise not to keep him long. It's a personal matter that requires discretion." She looked at Lady Atwood, who apparently had no idea who she was or why she needed to speak with Neville. Deferring to him, she asked permission.

"Shall I go for a moment, Neville?"

"Yes, dear. Give us a few moments. I'm afraid I don't want your delicate ears to hear a conversation that may turn out to be most unpleasant."

Lady Atwood gave a quick curtsy and wandered over to the refreshments table. Jane turned her ire on Neville.

"What did you say to Matthew?" she demanded. "He has abandoned me, suddenly announcing that his regiment has called him back to active duty to fight Napoleon. I saw you speaking with him earlier."

"I wasn't aware until now either that he had been recalled, but perhaps it's for the best," Neville replied. "You were about to discard him anyway, weren't you?" His flashed an accusatory stare in her direction. "The talk of the ton is the Duke of Wharton's invitation for you to be his mistress."

"How in the hell did you find out about that?" she growled.

"Men talk over port as much as women gossip over tea," Neville replied nonchalantly. "Do you deny the rumor that he has his eye on you?"

Jane thought carefully about the predicament she suddenly found herself in, and to her horror, she felt as if she were drowning in a deep lake. Yes, it was true. The duke had made an offer, and she seriously pondered it. Though she swore in the past that she would not be a kept woman under any circumstance, her father had cut her allowance severely upon learning of her association with Matthew. The old man puffed and kept his threat, and as a result, Jane had fallen into financial difficulties which Matthew knew nothing about.

She had two choices. One, to relent to the tugging of her heart concerning Matthew, or two, to accept the offer of the duke who would lavish her gifts and support her lifestyle. Although the duke had married for convenience, he sought comfort and refuge in the arms of another. Jane's reputation piqued his interest. Since he was somewhat appealing, wealthy, and titled, Jane considered it time to move on from the temptation to surrender to love. Each day in Matthew's arms turned into a battle to suppress her amorous feelings for him. She admitted her motive to accept the duke's proposal was terribly superficial, for her own self-gain and preservation, but she needed to survive and adapt.

"I do not deny the offer has been made," she replied. "Although I have not accepted his suggestion, it appears Matthew has given me no other choice."

Neville shook his head in disbelief. "Damn you, Jane." He narrowed his eyes in disdain. "You are a cold and heartless bitch," he spat out vehemently.

"I beg your pardon?" she replied, glowering at him after the insult.

"Matthew loves you, and you damn well know it," he said.

"As he finally voiced to me a few minutes ago, which I told him long beforehand that love was not an option."

"And you feel nothing for him after all this time? He has done everything he could to woo you back into his arms, seek your forgiveness for what he put you through nine years ago, and to make you his wife as it should have been. I told him it was a waste of time." Neville shook his head.

"I think highly of him," Jane replied in her defense. "Since I haven't cast him aside, but he has me, then why should you call me a heartless bitch?"

"Well, if he gets killed in battle, you can blame yourself for his sad end. He will have left this world with a broken heart," Neville shot back in anger, his nostrils flaring. "Now, if you'll excuse me, I have a real lady waiting for me that needs my attention."

As Neville hastily departed, his words pricked Jane's heart. *If he gets killed in battle, you can blame yourself for his sad end.*

She brought her hand to her throat, suppressing a sob that bubbled up from inside her soul. The reaction caught Jane by surprise, triggering the room to spin as if she would faint. Never in a thousand years would she wish Matthew to die so horribly. The thought of it made her tremble. She saw a nearby empty chair and quickly sat down. As she attempted to regain her wits, Millicent came to her side.

"Jane, are you unwell?" she asked, placing her hand on Jane's shoulder. "Where is Matthew?"

"Gone," she replied, her voice trembling.

"What do you mean, gone?"

"He's been called back to active duty to fight Napoleon." She gazed up at her aunt, whose astonishment showed in her widened eyes. "What am I to do, Auntie? He's left me again."

"Oh dearest," she moaned. "I'm so very sorry."

Chapter 21

∽ Surrender to the Inevitable ∽

Matthew stormed from the Westlake residence and walked blindly into the night. Filled with rage and hurt, he wanted nothing more than to leave London and never return. The decision he had made at the spur of the moment abruptly changed his path. In his gut, he knew that it had been the right thing to do. Because of Jane, his focus had clouded in a failed attempt to rectify the past. Finally, he arrived at the realization that he could not make amends for what transpired nine years ago, nor could he change the woman Jane had become. Perhaps he was right—it had been her choice, and he need not bear the totality of guilt. He had wasted enough time in her bed, and now it was time to make nobler choices.

If by some miracle he returned from battle, he would settle down with his father at Rutland Park and pursue a young debutante next season. Neville had done well for himself, so surely Matthew too could pull out the claws that Jane had sunk into his heart and find comfort elsewhere. He prayed a shred of friendship with Neville would be salvaged as he needed Neville's support to stay firm in his resolve. When and if Matthew returned, he would avoid Jane rather than be tempted again to folly. He had been a blind fool. She had used him—he had used her. The companionship had been doomed from the onset.

Although his father would be sorely disappointed and filled with worry about his recall to active duty, Matthew promised to sell his commission and resign once the conflict concluded. If he ended up dead on the battlefield, then in the afterlife he would reunite with Felicity and spend eternity with her. The thought brought an odd sense of comfort to him amidst the turmoil of his soul.

The next morning, Matthew made no haste in leaving his flat in London. He bid farewell to his father at Rutland Park. The regiment planned to move out in a matter of days, and he was more than ready to resume his duties.

Since he would all but disappear and return to the nearby barracks and his officer's quarters, Jane would find it difficult to reach out to him. A part of him hoped that she would suddenly realize she loved him, but he was not so foolish as to hold on to that delusion. He fully believed she had accepted the duke's offer and moved on, not giving him a second thought except for perhaps their moments of intimacy. He wondered if he had been the first in a long line of lovers to walk away and hoped a slight wounding of her female ego had resulted from his abrupt departure.

The day before shipping out, he received word of a visitor. Neville had called, and for the sake of their friendship, Matthew agreed to see him. Dressed in full uniform, he appeared far different from their last conversation. As Neville entered his quarters, he halted at the doorway, wide-eyed.

"I'm not sure if I should salute you or offer a handshake," Neville smirked. "Good God, Matthew, even I am intimated by the look of you."

Matthew grinned in delight. "A handshake with an old friend is sufficient," he said, offering his. "You're lucky to have caught me as we leave at first light in the morning."

Neville gave a hearty handshake in return. "I could not let you go without seeing you," he admitted.

"I'm glad you did," Matthew said, full of nostalgia over their past. "We've known each other for some time. It's grieved me of late that we've drifted apart, but I take full responsibility for that occurrence due to my foolhardiness." He pointed to a nearby chair. "Sit awhile."

Neville took an empty chair, and Matthew leaned against his desk, smiling warmly at his friend. "How is your Lady Atwood doing? Have you set a date?"

"I've yet to go down on bent knee, but soon, I hope. You will be the best man, of course, so I fully expect you to return."

"I'd be honored," Matthew admitted. "But war is fickle, as you well know, so I make no promises."

Matthew could speak of the possibility of his death without fear. He had come to that acceptance before on the battlefield, and this time he was able to embrace the likelihood much easier. Perhaps the knowledge that Felicity waited on the other side had been the comfort. She loved him, and he had loved her. If heaven existed, nothing would be lost.

"I'll be honest, Matthew," Neville began. "My gut tells me that your life will be long, so I fully expect your return."

"Always the optimist." Matthew grinned.

Neville lowered his head and fiddled with the rim of his hat in his hand. Matthew knew he wanted to bring up another subject, and as much as it pained him, he chose to allow her name to leave his lips.

"Have you spoken with Jane since my departure?" Matthew asked, showing no outward emotion. Inwardly, his gut tightened in sorrow.

"Not since the ball when I last spoke with you," Neville admitted. "However, I've received a communication from Lady Whitmore that Jane is distraught and would appreciate my intervention."

"Intervention for what?" Matthew balked.

"Apparently, her aunt has concerns about her accepting the duke's proposal. Disturbing reports are floating around the ton that he possesses a volatile temper."

"And what has that to do with me?" Matthew replied, furrowing his brow. "Jane is capable of making her own decisions regarding what males she allows in her bed. You know as well as I do that she will not listen to reason."

"Yes, I'm well aware the woman has a mind of her own." Neville sighed. "Her aunt told me, however, that her father has restored her allowance, so she may not take the duke's offer."

"I don't understand."

"You weren't aware that he nearly cut off her financial support?"

"She never spoke of it," Matthew admitted.

"Well, apparently, it was because she insisted on maintaining her companionship with you, and he vehemently opposed the arrangement. She became desperate with her dwindling funds and considered the duke's proposal so she would have a provision."

Matthew shook his head. "God, her reasoning is beyond my comprehension. I would have helped her financially or even married the woman, given her a home, and taken care of her the rest of her life." His nostrils flared in anger. "You would think that one day that stone heart of hers would crack and allow someone to love her." He raised his voice in frustration.

"You gave a good go of it, Matthew," Neville replied. "More so than I did."

"It's my fault. You warned me, as the others did, and I thought if it ever came to it, I'd be able to forget Jane easily regardless." He released a long, drawn-out sigh.

"You haven't, though, and you still love and want her, probably more than ever," Neville stated.

"Well, that is my folly and burden to bear. I have other things to worry about such as dodging bullets and bayonets. Undoubtedly, I shall not allow myself to become some lovesick weakling while attempting to preserve my life in battle." Matthew shook his head over his stupidity. "So help me, if I survive this conflict, I'll find myself another young lady and settle down."

Neville rose to his feet. "Well, friend, I wish you Godspeed. You shall be in my thoughts and prayers."

"Thank you," Matthew said, shaking his hand again. "Do a favor for me?"

"Yes, I'll keep my eye on her from a distance," Neville answered, already knowing the question.

"Thank you. And Father too. I worry about him."

"Of course. Whatever you ask." Neville put his hat back on and readied to leave. "When you're done ridding the world of Napoleon, I shall return to Rutland Park to congratulate you," he said.

"I look forward to it. By that time, I will have sold my commission. I have promised Father no more heroics. He's aging, and I have duties to attend to at Rutland Park."

"Glad to hear of it," Neville replied. "Take care of yourself."

Matthew watched his friend depart, leaving him behind to face his fate, grateful they had parted on good terms.

CHAPTER 22

∽ Sudden Farewells ∽

Jane read the words penned by Lord Byron, remembering Matthew's unexpected goodbye. *"All farewells should be sudden when forever."*

Admittedly, the moment he decided to leave after his announcement his intention had been forever. He had returned to war, and the fact that he could be killed weighed heavily upon Jane's heart.

She read in the paper that Matthew's regiment had left for the Continent to join the Prussian forces. The thought of him going to battle raged in her mind daily as if she were a party to the conflict itself. His absence opened an unobstructed door to replace him with the duke, who had already begun to hound her for a private moment together.

As she carefully considered what to do about it, her aunt made her concerns known about the duke's reputation. After promising to be careful, Jane threw all caution to the wind and invited him behind her closed doors at her town house to decide about pursuing a future as his mistress.

Frankly, she had tired of companions one after another who sought her heart and hand in marriage. Becoming a mistress of an important man did have its advantages, both monetarily and personally. However, her own conditions remained—no love and no children.

Jane didn't realize how raw her emotions had become over Matthew's departure until she opened the door to the duke. His carriage, with the family crest on the door and its fine horses, remained outdoors in front of her home. No doubt the neighborhood would take note of his visit.

"Your Grace, please come into my humble abode," Jane said.

He pulled off his hat, then removed his gloves and stuffed them inside. "No butler?" he remarked.

"None, Your Grace. Here, let me take those for you." She placed his hat on a side table in the foyer, and he scowled at her servitude.

"Well, this will not do. If we are to solidify our arrangement, you'll be set up in a proper town house with servants, including a butler, maids, and a cook."

His eyes glanced around her surroundings, appearing unimpressed. Not quite sure what the man expected, she found her first observation of his character disheartening.

"May I offer you a drink?" Jane asked, leading him into her parlor, which suddenly felt extremely inadequate. "A glass of port, perhaps?"

"Yes, if you don't mind," he replied, sitting down in Jane's overstuffed chair like the king of her domain.

He took the drink in hand, taking small sips. Jane sat down across from him with a sense of uneasiness flowing through her veins. By the jitters in her nerves, she concluded that the pursuit of another male in her life might have come too soon. She had barely taken time to shake Matthew from her consciousness and now sat across from a domineering man with one intent in his eyes. The thought of sharing a bed with him made her queasy. After all, as with any other potential mate, she needed time to build up the anticipation and enjoy the foreplay of seduction. The duke held a different idea of how soon he wished to take her. By the look in his eyes, it would be any minute now.

"So, I've read the colonel has returned to the front to fight Napoleon," he remarked coolly. "A timely departure, don't you think?" He pulled up one side of his mouth in a malevolent smirk.

"Timely for you perhaps," Jane coyly replied. "A bit of a shock to me, frankly, as I was unaware that he could be called back to active duty."

"You'd think he would have had enough of heroics after all these years, but some men feed upon the thrill of the military." The duke took a drink and eyed her bodice. "I, on the other hand, find the thrill of the hunt more my taste."

"I'm sure you do," Jane replied. "Not all men are called to heroics."

His eyes darkened at her comment, and he motioned to her with his finger. "Come here and sit on my lap," he ordered.

"The chair is a bit small for two," Jane protested with a snicker.

"Now, now, you've invited me into your home, Lady Jane. Where is your hospitality?"

Jane knew the duke would not relent, so she slowly rose to her feet and walked over to him. He patted his thigh, and she sat down, putting her arm around his shoulder. At first, she found no aversion to his appearance. Though he still emanated social snobbery, he was attractive. She decided to relax and enjoy the expected purpose of the evening. Before she decided, she wanted to taste the goods as much as he did.

"Now that wasn't bad, was it?" He gulped the remainder of his glass and set it down on a small table next to the chair. Afterward, he took his finger and placed it under her chin, lifting it up slightly. Looking down upon her, he gazed at her lips and then kissed her softly. It did not take long for his other hand to touch the bodice of her dress to fill his palm with her rounded breast. "You are a well-endowed woman," he remarked. "I shall enjoy the comfort."

"Thank you, Your Grace," Jane replied as her body became aroused at his touch. "I am known for giving great comfort."

"I've heard," he remarked.

The duke removed his hand from her breast and began tugging at the fabric of her skirt. As he pulled it upward, Jane squirmed at the anticipation of his destination. He stopped at her inner thigh, and teasingly kissed her, inserted his tongue in her mouth. A moment later, he inched up a bit farther and halted. Then with precision, he touched her moist body and groaned as he inserted a finger into her vagina. Realizing it was impossible to stop him now, she suggested they retire.

"Why don't we go to my bedroom where we can be more comfortable," she proposed.

He released her, and Jane rose to her feet. "This way," she directed, using her index finger to call him toward her. Heated and aroused, Jane saw his countenance darken with anticipation. The look was not one she had seen before in a man's eyes, and she wondered what new experience awaited.

By the time they reached her bed, the duke swiftly stripped her naked with little foreplay or affection. A second later, he rid himself of his garments, baring his chest. To Jane's surprise, he kept a rather attractive physique. Instead of removing his boots and trousers, he unbuttoned the frontal flap and pulled out his bulging erection. In a quick movement, he pushed her down upon the bed and spread her open with his knee in a forceful advance.

"Your Grace," she remarked. "Wouldn't you rather take time to get to know one another? Foreplay perhaps?"

He said nothing and looked wickedly at her with burning lust. As he began to position himself to enter her body, it dawned on her that he wore no sheath. Everything had happened so fast, Jane did not have the opportunity to speak about spilling his seed elsewhere. A flood of panic flashed through her body.

"Your Grace," she pleaded. "You must stop. I don't wish to get pregnant," she implored. "I have sheaths to use."

"I don't use them," he growled, nibbling on her lower lip to shut her up. "I'll send away any bastard children that come from our union."

Shocked at his cruel statement, Jane balled her fists and attempted to push him off. His body weight pressed her firmly into the mattress, and his large frame spread her legs apart uncomfortably.

"Feisty one," he said, grabbing her wrists with both his hands and pinning her down. "I enjoy rough foreplay and taking what I want."

"Get off me!" Jane bellowed. The duke repositioned himself, attempting to thrust himself into her at any second. She attempted to wiggle from underneath, but he kept her pinned as his prisoner. Since she could not escape or beat him away with her wrists wrapped by his hands, she did the unthinkable, and spit in his face. Her saliva hit him on his mouth and chin, surprising herself that her aim had been so proficient.

"You fucking bitch!" he railed, bringing his hand to his mouth to wipe off her dribble.

The duke exploded into a tirade that sent shivers down Jane's spine. He leaped from the bed, taking his handkerchief and wildly wiping the drool as if she had infected him with a fatal disease. The next moment, he turned red in the face, screaming obscenities as he towered above her lying in the bed.

"I should horsewhip you for that," he shrieked. A second later, he raised his hand as if he were about to strike her across the cheek but relented. Fearful he would beat her, Jane jumped out of bed and stood on the opposite side, putting distance between them.

"I told you to stop and you wouldn't," she yelled in return. "I am not an animal to rut without thought. You act like a beast."

"Who do you think you are?" he growled, narrowing his eyes at her. The duke took an angry step to the foot of the bed. "You're nothing but the ton's whore, going from man to man as if you can do what you want."

"And what if I am?" she replied, feeling shame drench her like rain. "At least I'm not a kept woman, and I sure as hell will not be yours." She grabbed a sheet off the bed and wrapped it around her body. "Get out of my house," she ordered, pointing at the door.

Rather than obeying, Jane saw him take another angry step and halt. A coldness ran down her spine as she saw the intent in his eyes to bodily harm her. Terror shot through Jane as she witnessed his closed fists, clenched teeth, and the darkness in his eyes. Frantically, she reached over to the nightstand, opened the drawer, and grabbed a dagger. She had placed it there years ago in case something like this happened but never thought she would have to use it. With a trembling hand, she brandished it at him.

"Take one more step, and so help me, I'll shove this in your chest," she growled. "Get out of my home now!"

After looking at the tip of the sharp object pointed toward him, the duke retreated. "You fucking bitch," he railed, grabbing his clothes from the floor and dressing in haste. "You're finished in this town," he growled like a bear. "By the time I get done smearing your name, there won't be another man from here to Hades that will have anything to do with you. You will be spurned at every social function in London and branded a common prostitute. Mark my word."

Jane stood her ground but inwardly trembled as she pointed the dagger in his direction. A moment later, he departed and slammed the door on the way out of her residence. She followed his exit downstairs and quickly locked the barrier. A second later, she put the dagger down on the foyer table, and brought both hands to her face and shuddered. The duke had nearly violated her and would have surely raped her if she hadn't stopped him. No man had dared to call her a whore to her face before, and the suggestion stuck a vein of remorse in her chest. Her scandalous behavior had finally delivered its consequences.

For years, she had considered her choice of men as her own entertainment to fill the lonely, aching need in her soul. She enjoyed the company of gentlemen and more than amply enjoyed the benefits of sexual pleasure. Nonetheless, for the first time in years, Jane saw herself as if she had left her body and beheld the truth. She loathed the woman she had become—a pathetic, hard-hearted creature who had let the past mold her into a wretched human being.

Nauseated by the awareness of her existence, she ran to her bath chamber and emptied the contents of her stomach. Afterward, an overwhelming ache for Matthew came from deep within her soul. She had yearned for his love for years, and now that she finally had it in her grasp, like an utter fool, she had let it go.

"How pitiful I am," she cried. "I've lost him again."

Chapter 23

∽ Victory at Waterloo ∽

In late July, the Duke of Wellington had led the Anglo-Dutch-German armies to victory. Alive but slightly wounded from the slice of a bayonet on his upper thigh, Matthew had avoided the death angel once again. With renewed purpose, he sold his commission as he had promised his father and returned to Rutland Park in late September.

Away from society and his friends, he had taken time to redirect his heart toward the hope of nobler pursuits rather than using Jane for pleasure. The more he considered what he had done, the angrier he became with himself for accepting her proposal of companionship. The time he had spent with Jane had robbed him of dignity, blinding him in the pleasure of her flesh and his reckless entanglement to win her heart. As the bayonet had slit his thigh, he felt assured once he returned to England that he successfully had eradicated her from his heart.

As Neville had done before, after Matthew returned home, he came to visit. With a singular purpose, Matthew determined to renew and cherish their friendship going forward. As soon as he saw Neville enter the room, a broad grin brightened his face.

"Matthew, I swear you're a man with nine lives," Neville said. Rather than offering a handshake, he threw his arm around Matthew and gave him a hug and a pat on the back. After showing his delight, he glanced down at his leg. "I heard they took a slice out of you. Nothing permanent, I hope."

"No, a clean cut, healing nicely," Matthew reported. "I will admit it shall leave a rather nasty-looking scar though."

"Ah, a battle scar for honor," Neville remarked. "I hear Wellington is awarding everyone a medal of honor for their participation at Waterloo. Another for your collection, no doubt."

"Not quite. The medal is for the noncommissioned officers and soldiers who engaged in battle. Well deserved," Matthew remarked proudly. "My collection shall go in my drawer," he noted, feeling uneasy about the attention. "I've sold my commission, and I'm a mere civilian now."

"Well, thank goodness." Neville sighed in relief. "Then your first order of business is to be my best man. I'm getting married next month," he announced with a joyful sing-song voice.

"Congratulations! The young lady accepted. Then we need to toast to your upcoming nuptials." Matthew walked over to the decanter of port. After pouring two glasses and handing one to Neville, he raised the other. "I wish you much happiness with your new bride."

"Thank you," Neville said. They drank and took seats across from one another.

"So, what are your plans now that you have returned?" Neville asked.

Matthew took a sip and settled comfortably into the chair. "There's much to be done here at Rutland Park. There are portions of the house that my father has neglected. It needs repair," Matthew noted a crack in the plaster above their heads. "My last tour of duty did not do him well. Upon my return, even after a few months, he appeared frailer than I care to see him."

"Sorry to hear of it," Neville said.

For a few moments, they fell into a digestive silence, and Matthew's mind wandered to the one topic that always seemed to rise between them whether he wanted it to or not. As much as he believed he had rid himself of lingering emotions where Jane had been concerned, he couldn't help but wonder if she had taken up with the duke during his absence. It would have been the next natural course of action. Neville must have noticed his furrowed brow and musing mind and offered to open the discussion.

"Shall I speak the name?" He arched a curious brow.

"Just tell me if she's well. That's all I need to know," Matthew replied, taking a gulp of alcohol.

"She's left London, Matthew."

Thinking that the duke had set her up elsewhere, he responded with no great surprise. "Did the duke buy her a residence?"

"She's not with the duke," Neville flatly replied. "From what I gather, she discovered a dark side to his personality at their first meeting and decided not to pursue the relationship."

Surprised and relieved in the same breath, Matthew asked the obvious. "Then where did she go?"

"She's living in her aunt's town house in Bath. As far as I know, she intends on staying there permanently, having tired of London."

"I find that surprising," Matthew admitted. "Has she found another companion?"

Neville's face turned pensive. After taking a sip of his drink, his brow furrowed before he spoke.

"Jane's spurning of the duke had a ripple effect, the consequences of which were not pleasant. He began spreading lies about her taking money for sex, calling her nothing more than a common whore, embarking on a campaign to ruin her beyond measure."

The news caused the hairs on the back of Matthew's neck to rise. The vindictiveness of the duke's actions angered him deeply. "Did he implicate you, me, or others as providing her those funds?"

"Not directly, but I quickly put a stop to the rumors as much as I could. In fact, I approached the duke and had a rather terse conversation that nearly led to blows. Having heard a few unsavory rumors myself regarding his character, I threatened him with retaliating tales of my own to circulate if he didn't cease spreading lies about Jane."

"I see," Matthew replied. "A kind action on your behalf."

"Jane, on the other hand, from what her aunt tells me, has gone through a rather dramatic awakening of sorts, so she's left society indefinitely."

Matthew gulped the rest of his glass, confused over his statement. "I don't quite understand what you're referring to as an awakening of sorts."

"Her aunt says she has regrets for the past."

Matthew shifted uncomfortably in his chair as Neville stared at him intently, waiting for a reaction. Matthew could only scoff at the suggestion. "I find that hard to believe," he dismissed. "What brought on that extraordinary change of heart?"

Neville held out his glass. "I need a refill."

Matthew obliged and walked over to the decanter, refilling both their glasses. He contemplated Neville's comments about Jane having regrets but doubted any sincerity on her part. By his skeptical reaction, he knew that his own heart had hardened against her for protection.

Matthew did not wish to think that her misgivings had anything to do with him. After handing the glass back to Neville, he sat down.

"Well, she has no regrets over me," Matthew affirmed as if to convince himself. "Perhaps the rumors the duke had started pricked her conscience in some fashion."

"Oh, she has regrets, Matthew, and according to her aunt, there are profound regrets where you are concerned."

Matthew waved his hand as if to flick off the news like a fly. "I don't wish to hear about it. My course is set, and I shall be pursuing a wife elsewhere." Rather than argue, Neville remained thoughtful. A moment later, Sir Charles entered the room.

"Viscount, how good it is to see you," he said, shuffling over to Neville to greet him. Arthritis in his knees and feet had worsened to such a point it left pain with each movement.

Neville rose to his feet. "Good to see you as well." He offered a handshake and then glanced at Matthew. "At last he's home for good, and I'm sure you are thankful again for his safe return."

"Indeed, I am." Matthew's father moved stiffly over to a chair and slowly sat down. "Damn arthritis," he cursed. "It's taken its toll upon me these past months as the cooler weather sets in."

"I noticed," Neville said. Without pausing for a breath, he cleverly suggested, "You should take the waters at Bath. I've been told they do wonders."

Matthew shot a disgruntled look in his friend's direction. As he was about to open his mouth and protest the conversation, Neville continued.

"The mineral waters do wonders for the joints. You should definitely bathe in the waters for relief."

"You know, I hadn't thought about that," Sir Charles remarked. "What say you, Matthew?" His father glanced at him with a perky hopefulness in his gaze. "A trip to Bath now that you are home would do us both good. You can relax and rejuvenate. Perhaps it will aid the healing of your leg wound."

"Father, the trip is long, and I daresay it will do you more harm to sit in a carriage for days while we travel." Matthew attempted to discourage his father. He glanced over at Neville, knowing exactly why he had suggested the idea, and scowled.

"I'll be fine, Matthew. The waters will do me wonders. This is the first good suggestion I've heard in months." He pondered for a moment and then grinned at Neville. "Why don't you come with us, Viscount? We can make a holiday of it, the three of us."

"Yes, Neville. Since this was your idea, I insist you come with us," Matthew pressed him, sounding a bit snide in tone. He pulled his mouth into a lopsided grin, playing his own shrewd game.

"Well, sir, I'm about to be married next month," Neville announced, swiftly excusing himself. "Poor timing, I'm afraid."

"Then you had best take a holiday, young man, before you tie yourself down to marital life. Isn't that right, Matthew?"

"Oh, definitely," Matthew agreed, nodding his head. He reveled in the opportunity to drag Neville along out of spite. "A holiday is just what he needs before taking his vows." He paused for a moment. "Does your family still use their town house in Bath?"

"Yes." He sighed. "It's vacant, so you are more than welcome to stay with me." He exhaled a puff of air from his lungs in defeat.

"Good. Then it's settled. Let us leave in two days. My aching joints are anxious to find relief."

"Two days," Matthew concurred.

"Well, I'll leave you to some privacy," his father replied, wobbling to his feet. After he shuffled out the door, Matthew glared at Neville.

"Are you attempting to put me in Jane's path again?" he grumbled in a low tone, knowing damn well that was his strategy.

Neville smiled warmly as a concerned friend. "My gut tells me there is still unfinished business between the two of you."

"Bollocks," Matthew harshly replied. "I have said all I needed to say to her. It's over between us."

"Perhaps, but I sense she has things to say to

you. Stop complaining," he urged. "Are we taking your carriage or mine to Bath?"

"Definitely yours," Matthew demanded. "It's more comfortable."

"Mine it is then." Neville sighed, rising to his feet.

Matthew stood too. "I suppose I should thank you for accommodating Father and me at your town house as guests."

Neville grinned. "How could I refuse that cunning move on your part? Well played." Neville headed for the foyer and halted at the front entrance. "I suppose I shall go home and tell my fiancée that I've been called away for a few days."

Matthew halted at the door and shook his head in disbelief. "I cannot believe that you have tricked me into going to Bath by using my father's condition to your advantage."

"You're not the only one who knows military tactics," Neville spouted. "I have a few tricks up my own sleeve as well."

"Touché," Matthew replied in defeat. The idea of seeing Jane gave him a headache.

Chapter 24
∽ Healing Waters ∽

They arrived in Bath, and Sir Charles took no time visiting the healing waters for his aching joints. After a few dips, he swore that he felt ten years younger. Matthew doubted it, of course, but humored him anyway. Perhaps the heavy mineral content in the springs did help to some extent. Matthew feared, however, once they returned to the damp and cold Rutland Park, the arthritis would come back. It saddened him that his father had to deal with the pain.

On the second day of their arrival, a note arrived from Lady Whitmore, inviting Neville and Matthew to afternoon tea. When Matthew read the invitation, he knew that Jane would be there. The thought of seeing her tightened every muscle in his stomach more so than facing death on the battlefield. Neville had continued attempting to convince him that he needed to meet with her one more time before putting a lid on the coffin, so to speak, of their relationship.

"I don't know what you expect me to do," Matthew argued as their carriage came to a halt in front of Lady Whitmore's residence.

"You don't need to do anything. I'm not forcing you, for heaven's sake, to make amends with the woman."

"Make amends? I have no apologies to confess," he shouted indignantly. "If anyone needs to make amends, it's her."

"Well, maybe she will. People change, you know."

"Doubtful," Matthew swiftly rebuffed, exiting the carriage. Neville led the way while Matthew lagged behind. After a few raps of the knocker, the door opened, revealing Lady Whitmore's butler. Neville presented his calling card.

"Viscount Berkshire to see Lady Whitmore," he said.

"Do come in. Her ladyship is waiting for you in the parlor."

Neville entered, and Matthew stood on the stoop, hesitating. He did not want to be near Jane, feeling as if he were about to face a firing squad for cowardice. One look into her eyes and all reason would fly away. Even before he stepped into her presence, he sensed the unmistakable power that she held over his heart. Neville glanced over his shoulder.

"Are you coming?" He narrowed his eyes, giving Matthew a cautionary warning not to embarrass him by retreating.

"Yes," Matthew tersely replied, stepping into the foyer. The butler led them a few feet down, and they turned to the right and entered a large parlor that sat with tall windows facing the street.

"Ah, gentlemen," Lady Whitmore said, rising to her feet. "Do come in. How kind of you to accept my invitation for tea."

Matthew quickly noted Jane's absence, which allowed him to exhale the breath he had been holding. After bowing and giving her ladyship a kiss on her hand, they took seats. Lady Whitmore poured a cup for each of them, and they went through the motions of answering the usual questions regarding milk and sugar. Uncomfortable, Matthew found it difficult to focus on Lady Whitmore. He caught himself continually glancing at the parlor threshold, waiting for Jane to enter at any moment.

"Colonel, it is so good to see you safely home," Lady Whitmore said, starting a conversion. "I heard you were wounded, but you appear quite recovered."

"Yes, your ladyship. A slight slice of a bayonet, but it's healed now."

"And your father, I understand, is taking the waters. Is it helping his arthritis?"

"He tells me so." At a loss for polite conversation, Matthew took a sip of tea. Thankfully, Neville filled the silence.

"And you, Lady Whitmore. How have you been?"

"Oh, just fine. I could not wait to leave London and get away. This season has not been the best for me. I am getting too old for all the gossip and nighttime soirees, balls, and dinner parties. After all, I'm not looking for a husband, am I?"

She laughed at her quip, and Matthew and Neville did as well.

"But do tell, Viscount. You are about to be married to Lady Atwood. How delightful. A wonderful girl. You have done well for yourself."

"Thank you," Neville said, smiling with pride. "I am very fond of the young lady."

"Fond," she chortled. "I daresay you look absolutely lovestruck." She shook her finger at him. "Admit it!"

Neville squirmed at Lady Whitmore's playful prodding but confessed to her accusation. "You are quite right. I'm hopelessly in love." He modestly lowered his head. "Frankly, I thought I would never love again, but alas, cupid has struck me with his arrow."

"See, now, that wasn't so hard." She picked up a plate of finger sandwiches. "May I offer you a treat?"

Neville, apparently eager to stuff his mouth rather than talk, snatched a cake.

"Colonel?"

Matthew shook his head. "No, thank you." When he glanced at the empty entranceway again, she put the plate down.

"I surmise by your constant glimpse at the door you are seeking my niece," she said. "If you wish to speak with Jane, she will receive you in the solarium. It's down at the end of the hall and a sharp turn to your right."

"Well, I . . . " Matthew did not know how to react.

"It's up to you, Colonel. She will respect your choice whether to speak with her or not."

Neville gave him a slight nudge with his elbow. "Unfinished business," he said in a low tone. "Do not put aside the chance."

Matthew was not quite sure how or why he found himself standing. Unexpectedly, there he was, walking toward the doorway, following the hall to the sun parlor. The sensation was bewitching and troubling, but he had to gaze upon her one more time. Whatever needed to be finished between them, it had to be done or he would never find peace.

He came to the entrance and halted. Jane sat in a wicker chair, dressed in a blue afternoon dress with lace trim, holding a book in her hands. The sun streamed down on her through the windows above, forming shimmering waves on her hair. She looked different—demure, peaceful, and stunningly beautiful. It took a few seconds before she noticed him staring at her in awe. When she lifted her head, a slow smile brightened her face.

"Matthew." She put the book down and rose to her feet. "I'm glad that you decided to speak to me."

Her demeanor had dramatically altered.

Gone in her gaze was the haughty woman who reveled in her scandalous ways. Instead, here stood a beautiful creature who astounded him. His eyes wandered down her frame and suddenly halted as he saw the rounding of her abdomen. The blood drained from his face.

"Good God," he choked out. "You're pregnant." His throat closed at the shock. Jane roved her hand over the tiny bump as she looked at him with a sheepish grin. "Yes, I am pregnant."

"How—how?" Matthew sputtered, gasping for air.

Jane spoke in a low tone. "Do you remember the evening I was rather naughty, asking you for a different approach?" she asked with her cheeks turning a pink blush.

"How could I forget?" he remarked, gawking at her in disbelief that she was both pregnant and embarrassed.

"You had taken off the sheath and discarded it without noticing it had ripped on one side."

"I don't recall," he admitted, gaping at her pregnant form. He never bothered to check after discarding one. "Are you sure that . . . ?"

Jane interrupted him. "You have every right to question whether the child is yours. I have had relations with no one else since you left me," Jane replied. "It appears all my rules and various ways to assure I did not get pregnant were not foolproof." She paused, lowering her eyes for a second. When she looked back to him, she spoke with firm confirmation in her voice. "I want you to know, Matthew, that I do not expect anything from you."

She studied him with an amorous gaze—one that Matthew had never seen before. It took his breath away, sending his heart into a rapid beat.

"I'm so glad you're home safe and sound," she added. "Does your wound hurt?" She glanced at his legs.

"No, my physical wound does not pain me," he answered. "But my soul does as I stand here before you." He brought his hand to his head, staring at her midsection. "My God, Jane. You're pregnant."

"Sit down," she offered in a kind tone. "Let us talk."

Matthew moved awkwardly toward a chair, half in awe and half in shock. Jane continued to glow in the sun that filtered through the glass above, but he sweated from the heat of the room and his prickly nerves. His fingers reached up to his cravat and loosened it so he could breathe.

"What does the doctor say?" Matthew asked in an anxious tone. "Is all well?" He couldn't help but ask since Jane had lost one child and his deceased wife another. The prospect of pregnancy frightened him to the core, and fear ran through his veins that another tragedy would come of it.

"Yes, all is well, Matthew. The baby grows," she said, looking down at herself with joy in her eyes. "I'm beginning to feel movement, and it's wonderful."

Movement. A small growing baby, warm and safe within her body. He had impregnated her again, but this time, all appeared well. "Jane, I don't know what to say," he admitted. Awestricken by the news, he wondered if Neville had been aware of her condition.

"Matthew, I want you to listen to what I have to say as if no child of ours grows in my womb. Can you do that—I mean separate the two, so you understand?"

"I will try," he half-heartedly admitted.

"Good."

Jane settled into a comfortable position, taking her hand off her rounded belly as if to draw his attention elsewhere. He looked into her eyes that radiated a welcomed kindness.

"When you left me, I pursued the duke's offer so I could abandon the pain I experienced over your abrupt departure. At the time, I did not realize that I was with child, though I had been late with my menses. It had happened before, so I took no concern early on."

"All right," Matthew said, thinking he needed to say something.

"The man turned out to be a brute. The first opportunity we were alone, I feared he would rape me. By the time he left my home, I was drenched in shame, which was a sensation that had eluded me for years. He called me a whore, and for the first time, I actually felt like one."

"I never thought you such," Matthew replied affectionately.

"And you never made me feel like one. All the time we were together, I felt protected and loved, which were gifts I didn't know how to receive or comprehend, for that matter." Jane's eyes watered, and her voiced trembled as she continued. "When you broke my heart nine years ago, I hardened mine to protect myself. No love—no children became my declaration. I wanted the companionship of men, and I enjoyed sexual relations, so I became the gregarious, scandalous lady of the ton. I made a name for myself and frankly had a good go of it for a while."

Matthew sat quietly listening to Jane's painful admission. For a fleeting moment, he questioned the truth of her words. However, as he gazed at her in awe and the profound change in her demeanor, he accepted her sincerity.

"I swore to myself that if you ever asked me to come back as your companion," Matthew firmly announced, "that I would turn you down without blinking an eye." He stared at her resolutely so she would understand where he stood.

"I have no intention of asking you to do so," Jane assured him. "In fact, I'm perfectly capable of raising our child alone. My aunt has promised her support, though my father is furious with you." She snickered. "You should avoid him at all costs."

Alone? He couldn't believe that she wanted to keep their child without his involvement. "You cannot believe that I would let you raise our child by yourself," Matthew sternly objected, setting his jaw. "There is only one clear course of action."

"To marry me?" Jane shook her head. "After how I've treated you, Matthew, you have no obligation to marry me. I'm ashamed of who I am and intend not to be a woman who uses men any longer." Her hand came to her abdomen again, and she smiled. "I have a higher calling now, one that I'm quite excited to pursue."

Jane paused and looked at him, and he saw the trembling of her lower lip as she spoke. "Can you ever forgive me?"

Matthew could not understand why she asked for forgiveness. If anything, he should confess his regrets. At that moment, he realized that he did not want to marry her because he had impregnated her again. No. He wanted to marry her because he could not live without her another second. If she rejected him, his life would be over. The thought sent shudders of fear he hadn't experienced even when facing a thousand rifles or bayonets pointed in his direction. The sensation was dreadful.

Jane wrung her hands together, waiting for his response. Moved by her actions, he reached out and grasped them tightly for reassurance.

"There's nothing to forgive," he replied, his

voice shaking. "If anything, you should forgive me for having left you nine years ago. It has taken me some time to own my complicity in how deeply it affected you."

"You may not believe this," Jane began, with a tear trickling down her cheek, "but my heart never stopped loving you, Matthew. That was my problem. I did not understand how to move on after losing our baby and then losing you. I never properly grieved the loss. For years, I buried that love rather than facing it, and when you returned, it wanted to resurrect from my heart anew. Instead of allowing its rebirth, I denied it life. I assure you that I have suffered sufficiently for it. I'm so sorry."

"Do you really love me?" he said astonished by her words.

She smiled at him and squeezed his hand in return. "I love you dearly, my wonderful and kind Matthew."

He closed his eyes, hearing her declaration. She had told him nine years ago of her love, pleaded with him to stay, but he had turned a blind eye and broke her heart.

"I love you, Jane. Marry me. Not because you have our child in your womb but because it's the unfinished business between us." He chuckled at that damn statement that echoed in his mind thanks to his friend.

"Ah, yes. Neville and his unfinished business observation," she remarked. "We should perhaps thank him for bringing us together."

"So, you will marry me?" Matthew pressed her for an answer.

"Yes, my darling. I will marry you."

Unable to control his desire any longer, Matthew leaned forward and kissed her gently on the lips. As he did so, clapping came from the doorway. Matthew and Jane turned and saw Millicent and Neville smiling at the two of them.

"Finally," Neville remarked. "I can stop hounding the two of you."

Matthew rose to his feet, and Jane followed. As the congratulatory remarks came from her aunt and Neville, Matthew reveled in the victory. Though he could not take credit on all fronts for how it turned out, he was thankful for the outcome nonetheless. He had captured Jane's heart.

Chapter 25

Finished Business

After his father had sufficiently doused himself in the waters at Bath, Matthew told him of his impending marriage to Jane. With Neville by his side, who was anxious to return to London and Charity, he made the announcement.

"Father, I have news," Matthew said as he stood in the parlor. His father lifted his eyes from the chair in which he sat reading the newspaper.

"What sort of news?" he asked, peeking over the top of his glasses at Matthew.

"I have asked Jane Cavanagh to marry me." The confession caused a broad smile to spread across Matthew's face, reliving the joy of her acceptance.

"And what did the young lady say?" he asked, showing no excitement over the announcement. His father folded the paper and laid it down on his lap.

"She has accepted."

Sir Charles pondered silently for a few moments and then rose to his feet. After taking a step in Matthew's direction, he halted and looked him sternly in the eye.

"Have you impregnated her again?"

Matthew's mouth gaped open, and he quickly glanced at Neville, who appeared equally surprised that his father had such knowledge. After taking precautions to keep that little secret from him for many years, Matthew was flabbergasted and forced to confess.

"How did you know?"

"I may be an old codger with arthritis, but my hearing is quite sharp," he replied. "I heard her father state the surprising fact through the parlor door when he visited, screaming at you about the gossip column."

"Oh Father," Matthew moaned. "I didn't want you to know."

"What happened to the baby? Did she lose it?" he pressed. His bushy eyebrows frowned.

Matthew lowered his eyes and shook and head affirmatively, unable to admit the sad affair.

"I see," his father said, glancing over at Neville. "And you were aware, no doubt."

"Not until recently, sir," he replied. "I'm afraid that even I was not privy to that event."

"Well, then." Sir Charles sighed. "That answers quite a few questions for me regarding what happened nine years ago."

"Father, let me explain," Matthew pleaded.

Sir Charles raised his hand in the air, halting his son. "Nothing to explain. I'm personally aware that your love for the military had no doubt entered into your decision to break with Jane." He narrowed his eyes at Matthew and pointedly asked in a gruff tone. "Well, tell me, son. Have you impregnated the poor girl again? Answer me."

Matthew glanced at Neville in the hopes of finding an ounce of strength to admit his folly. Instead of receiving any, Neville appeared slightly amused that Matthew's father had put him on the spot. Slowly, Matthew shifted his eyes to his father, inhaled a deep breath, and sheepishly told him the truth.

"Yes, sir. She's five months pregnant."

Sir Charles scowled. Neville said an encouraging word.

"Well, sir, at least you'll soon be a grandfather," he nervously chortled.

"Hmmm," he responded. "Five months. It appears that your activities to reacquaint yourself with Jane went far beyond a mere conversation."

Matthew wanted to defend himself and Jane, but he lacked enough justification to make it look any less scandalous.

"Is she marrying you because you got her pregnant, or does the woman love you?"

"She loves me," Matthew replied, attempting to sound assured and confident.

"And you? What about you, Matthew? Is this another bid to do what is right or do you truly love Jane?"

"Well, let me answer that question," Neville interjected. "The man is besotted with her, Sir

Charles. In fact, the past between the two of them has been healed and all set right."

A single brow rose over Sir Charles's right eye. He glanced over at Matthew, who quickly affirmed the statement.

"We are in love, Father. Deeply in love. I never thought that I would find another to fill my heart like Felicity, but I assure you that Jane has sufficiently healed my sorrow."

A small smile began to creep across Sir Charles's face, and Matthew's tension waned.

"Five months, you say?"

"Five months," Matthew said.

"Well, then when do you plan to marry the young lady? You will need to get a common license, and we'll have the vicar of our parish perform the ceremony without the reading of the banns."

"I would like to wed at Rutland Park in a private ceremony," Matthew suggested.

"And what of Jane's father? Are you going to ask him for her hand in marriage or forgo that formality lest he shoots you in the head as promised?" Sir Charles smirked in amusement.

"Jane and I will speak of it, but my good senses advise me to let him know after we are wed," Matthew said.

"Probably wise," Neville agreed.

"Then I give you my congratulations and blessings," Sir Charles announced. He placed his hand on Matthew's upper arm.

"Thank you, Father," Matthew replied, breathing a sigh of relief. "I hope you do not mind, but Jane and I would like to return to London so she may get her affairs in order."

"Am I to assume that you and Jane intend to live at Rutland Park?" his father asked with a hopeful glint in his eye.

"Of course we do, if you don't mind having a grandchild underfoot," Matthew said with a twinkle in his eyes.

"Not at all, son. Not at all." Sir Charles glanced at Neville. "Neville, I surmise that you are anxious to get back to your lovely bride-to-be."

"I am, sir. Very ready."

"Then we will return as soon as Jane is ready for the trip," he announced. "I do hope that she can travel in her condition."

Matthew understood his father's concern. After losing two children, he had pressed Jane for assurance that she would be able to bear the journey. He even suggested that she stay in Bath until the baby was born, but she disagreed.

"Jane assures me that she will be fine," Matthew said, hiding his own worries.

"I've spoken to the driver," Neville announced. "He shall endeavor to go around the potholes in the road."

"With three males to escort her back to London, I daresay the young lady will be fine," Sir Charles remarked.

"Well, then I shall inform Jane of our plans,"

Matthew announced.

"Please tell Jane that I am most pleased that she will be my daughter-in-law and that I'm overjoyed at the prospect of being a grandfather," Sir Charles requested of Matthew. "I want her to understand that my fondness remains, and she shouldn't be embarrassed about the circumstances."

"I will," Matthew replied. "It's very kind of you, Father." Moved by the compassion of his father's words, Matthew's hope for the future soared.

The only gnawing worries that he could not shake related to the impending birth of the baby. Having once witnessed the loss of his wife in childbirth and the grief of holding his stillborn son, a deep-seated fear haunted him amidst the joy of marrying Jane.

As his father returned to his chair and the newspaper, Neville invited him for a private word in his study. He closed the door, walked to the decanter, and poured Matthew a drink of brandy.

"Here, take this," he said, holding out the glass. "I can always tell when you need a drink."

Eager for the relief, Matthew took it to his lips and sipped. His mouth had dried from nerves, and even his hand trembled slightly in movement.

"Yes, you know my moods," Matthew admitted, taking a single chair and sitting down.

Neville sat on the edge of his desk, swirling

the liquor around in his glass as if he were looking for the right words to speak.

"I sense you are worried about the birth," he began, "and rightfully so after all you have endured."

"I am," Matthew admitted, scrunching his brow. "All I see in my mind is Felicity and my dead son in my arms." He gulped a large portion of the alcohol. "I can't get the images out of my head, Neville, and am terrified it will happen again." Embarrassed that his eyes welled with tears, Matthew brought his hand to his forehead. "I cannot imagine going through this once more," his voice cracked. "Losing Jane—losing a child."

"Listen, Matthew," Neville consoled in a kind voice. "Many women do very well in childbirth. Look at my sister, Julianne. You know how petite and fragile she appears outwardly. I think she had us all fooled because, from what I heard from the midwife, she had no trouble birthing her daughter." Neville laughed. "Aside from a few blood-curdling screams, her husband tells me."

Matthew lowered his hand and inhaled a deep breath, regaining control over his emotions. "I'm glad to hear of it," he remarked.

"As far as Jane goes, I see no problem. She's strong physically and in character, Matthew. All will go well. You'll see." Neville reached out and gave Matthew an encouraging pat on his upper shoulder. Afterward, he grabbed his empty glass and refilled it. "Now settle your nerves," he ordered. "We need to get packing and send Jane word of our imminent departure."

"You're right," Matthew admitted.

"What of Millicent," Neville asked. "Is she coming too?"

"No, she's decided to remain in Bath and will return a month before Jane is due to give birth."

"Well, good. Then the four of us in my comfortable carriage will have a fine trip back to Rutland Park. All will be well."

Matthew forced a painful grin. Outwardly, he attempted to agree with everything Neville proclaimed. Inwardly, he struggled.

"Damn this dread," he bellowed aloud. "I can face Napoleon's army with less fear than the birth of a baby."

"Well, where love is involved, there is often uncertainty," Neville commented with an assured tone. "Even I am a bit nervous about my upcoming nuptials. Regardless, I find it quite romantic."

Astounded at Neville's insight, Matthew saw a depth in his friend he had never noticed before. He knew him to be right. Love often did involve uncertainty, and one must be willing to embrace the inherent risks.

CHAPTER 26
Certainty of a Future

Matthew paced outside the door of the bedchamber, wearing a path in the rug. As he waited and worried, his mind recalled every moment he had spent with Jane in his lifetime. The first time he saw her at the assembly when they danced. Young, innocent, and pretty, he couldn't control himself the day he took her through the maze. He knew full well that they had made a dead-end turn, and he wasn't about to show her the way out until the folly of his youth learned the art of seduction. A pang of guilt remained inside his soul over what had transpired between them. But he, like Jane, had chosen a path, and those days were long gone.

After hearing a moan on the other side of the door, Matthew's pace increased. He shoved his fingers through his unruly hair, wondering why in the world at three o'clock in the morning her contractions had begun. Naturally, she had come to term with no complications. Although he was eternally grateful that he had the opportunity to watch the baby grow in her womb and feel it kicking, he still struggled with worry.

Five hours had passed. Matthew glanced at

his pocket watch, noting the time near eight o'clock. He continued his back-and-forth strides, living the present but recalling the past to keep his mind elsewhere.

The years in the military had made him ripe for love when he met Felicity. She too had been pretty, demure, and in love with him. He adored her also and married her with the hope of a future together but never considered that uncertainty loomed before him. It was only a notion Matthew anticipated on the battlefield, staring death in the eye. Never had he thought that the angel would visit his beloved wife. The spirit was unpredictable in his visitations, showing up to claim souls at the most innocent of moments.

"I'm not a praying man," Matthew babbled as he halted before the closed door. Another moan, louder than the last, met his hearing. Inside were Jane's aunt and a midwife, helping her through the uncertain hours ahead. "But perhaps it's time."

Matthew wrung his hands together, afraid that he would go mad. He halted as he saw his father shuffling down the hallway in his slippers and robe.

"Is it time?" he asked, glancing at the closed door.

"Yes. Jane went into labor five hours ago."

"Five hours," he exclaimed. "You should have awakened me."

"To pace along by my side?" Matthew

responded.

"Well, don't wear yourself out. It took your mother nine hours to birth you if my memory serves me right."

Matthew remembered Felicity and the horrible endless hours of contractions and the appalling loss of blood, pooling on the sheets. Something had gone terribly wrong. As he frowned over the memories, Sir Charles reached out and touched him on the shoulder.

"Matthew, stop worrying. You're going to make yourself ill and will be no good to Jane or the baby," he admonished. "Why don't you sit down in that chair over there, and I'll have someone bring you a hot cup of tea?"

"Yes, yes, you're right," he admitted. Another moan came from behind the door, louder than the last, and Matthew's eyes widened.

"Shall I send a message to Neville that the baby is on the way? I'm sure that he'll be glad to stand by your side for moral support," his father suggested.

"Neville?" Matthew said, pulling his eyes away from the door. "Yes, Neville. Please send for him."

"I will if you sit down," his father ordered, pointing at the chair.

Matthew plopped on the chair, lowered his head in his hands, and heaved a shaky breath. "All right, all right," he relented. Another rasping groan came from behind the door, louder than the last, and Matthew stared at the barrier. His father had departed to get tea and Neville, leaving him there to stare at the divide between him and Jane. Suddenly the door opened, and Millicent came out. She glanced around, saw him, and smiled.

"Won't be long now, Matthew. Jane asked me to tell you everything is fine and to stop your fussing," she announced. "Every once in a while, on a strong contraction, she does curse like a bloody sailor though," she laughed.

Matthew shot to his feet. "She's all right?"

"Yes, fine." Millicent put both her hands on his shoulders and pushed him back down on the chair. "Sit, will you? You're making me nervous."

Matthew obeyed and looked up at Millicent with a forlorn gaze. "Watch over her," he pleaded with a trembling voice. As the words left his lips, Jane bellowed a groan.

"Oh dear. I must return," Millicent said, turning on her heel. She opened the door and slammed it behind her, leaving Matthew alone.

A maid with a tray approached with a cup of tea. "Your father asked me to bring this to you," she announced.

"Don't want tea," he barked, jumping to his feet. "All I want is to know that my wife and baby are fine."

Matthew began to pace once more as the maid set the tray on a nearby hall table.

"I'll just leave it here for you," she said, scurrying back down the stairs.

Another half hour passed, increasing Matthew's fears. Jane's moans had turned to shrieks of pain. A blood-curdling scream came from Jane's throat, sounding like the last one that Felicity had roared before her spirit left her body. Matthew put his hands on the door and lowered his forehead on the wooden surface.

"Please God, please. Not again," he pleaded in earnest.

A moment later, he heard the cries of a baby, wailing from the other side. Unable to wait any longer, he turned the doorknob and entered the room uninvited. By the look on Millicent's face, she hadn't the courage to shoo him away.

There in the arms of the midwife lay a crying, breathing infant. Matthew glanced at Jane, who looked exhausted and drenched in sweat, but nonetheless alive and well.

"Come in Matthew and look," she said. "We have a son." Tears streamed down her cheeks. "A beautiful baby boy."

Matthew had not shed a tear since the day that Felicity and Benjamin passed from his life. They were tears of sorrow, but as he stood there, he realized that his cheeks bore the tears of joy. The midwife had finished cleaning the babe and swaddled him in a blanket.

"Would you like to hold him?" she asked.

Matthew thought of Benjamin, whose lifeless body had been the last baby he held. Today it would be different, and without hesitation, he reached out and took the child into his arms. Still crying over his abrupt arrival into this world, Matthew cradled him tenderly.

"Shush, now," he said, smiling at the lad. "All is well." The babe responded to his voice and stared up at him with his blue eyes, ceasing his wailing.

"Let me see our son," Jane blubbered.

Matthew walked over and lowered their child into her arms.

"He's gorgeous, isn't he, Matthew?"

"Yes, a fine young lad," he proudly replied.

"What shall we name him?"

"You could name him Neville," came a voice from the doorway.

"What are you doing here?" Jane asked, glancing up at Matthew.

"I'm afraid I was a bit of a nervous wreck, waiting in the hallway. Father sent for him," Matthew admitted.

"Well, I see that all is well," Neville said, grinning from ear to ear.

Millicent quickly caught him at the doorway. "Give them a moment of privacy, you snoop," she said. "Jane isn't presentable yet."

Sir Charles arrived as Millicent was about to close the door. "You have a fine grandson, and Jane is well," she announced.

"Thank God," he exclaimed.

The door closed, and Matthew realized that he needed to let the ladies tend to Jane and the baby. No doubt his father would be smoking cigars and having a drink with Neville.

"What shall we name him?" Jane asked again.

Matthew had thought about it for some time, mulling over various options. One particular name came to mind for days that meant valor and strength. "I had hoped to name him Bryce," he said.

"Bryce," Jane repeated, looking down at the baby in her arms. "Yes, I like it."

Millicent added her approval. "Lovely name." Afterward, she gave Matthew a stern gaze. "Time for you to go and let us tend to Jane."

"Yes, of course," he said, "but not before I do this." Matthew bent down and kissed his wife softly on the lips and then drew back, looking at her with so much love that he thought his heart would burst. "I love you, Jane. Thank you for giving me a son."

Jane smiled. "You're welcome, Matthew." Tears welled in her eyes. "I love you."

With great difficulty, Matthew left her bedside and his new son to join his father and Neville downstairs. By the time he had reached the parlor, they were already smoking and drinking as if they were the ones who had fathered the child.

"Congratulations!" Neville burst forth.

"Thank you."

"Proud of you, son," his father remarked, taking a seat with a drink in hand.

"Well, I'm next on the list," Neville announced. "Charity is pregnant."

"You don't say?" Matthew excitedly remarked.

"Yes, it appears I am about to be a father as well, Matthew, so I'm going to need your support when she goes into labor."

"Delightful," Sir Charles remarked. "Congratulations to you too." He raised his glass. "This calls for a toast."

Matthew glanced at Neville, who returned the smile of a dear friend. They raised their glasses together.

"To wives, babies, and husbands," Sir Charles said. "May your lives be filled with the certainty of love and joy for the remainder of your days."

"Hear, hear," Neville and Matthew replied as they took a sip of their drink with Sir Charles. Matthew's fear of the future vanished, and a sense of security, love, and long life filled his heart. The war had been won.

About the Author

With Russian blood on my father's side and English on my mother's, I blame my ancestors for the lethal combination of my DNA that influences my stories. Tragedy and drama might be found between the pages, but I eventually give readers a happy ending.

I live in the beautiful but rainy Pacific Northwest. My hobby (more of an obsession) is researching my English ancestry and expanding my family tree. To keep the memory of my ancestors alive, I often use their names in my novels or dedications.

My usual genre is historical fiction with romantic elements and historical romance set in the Victorian and Edwardian eras. My books include:

- ❖ The Price of Innocence (Permanently Free) – Book One of the Legacy Series
- ❖ The Price of Deception – Book Two of the Legacy Series
- ❖ The Price of Love – Book Three of the Legacy Series
- ❖ The Price of Passion – Book Four of the Legacy Series
- ❖ The Legacy Series Box Set (Books 1-4)

- ❖ The Phantom of Valletta (Featured in The Sunday Times, Malta in 2010)
- ❖ Dark Persuasion (2012 Finalist in the USA Best Book Awards for Romance)
- ❖ A Portrait of Perfection (A Dark Gothic Tale of Love and Betrayal)
- ❖ A Christmas Oath (2015 Christmas Novelette)
- ❖ A Christmas Mission (2016 Christmas Novelette)
- ❖ Lady Isabella (Ladies of Disgrace)
- ❖ Lady Grace (Ladies of Disgrace)
- ❖ Lady Charlotte (Ladies of Disgrace)
- ❖ Lady Jane (Ladies of Disgrace)
- ❖ Toil Under the Sun

Romance with a Kiss of Suspense (formerly under the pen name of Nora Covington)
- ❖ Thorncroft Manor
- ❖ Whitefield Hall
- ❖ Blythe Court
- ❖ Morland Park (Coming Soon)
- ❖ Romance with a Kiss of Suspense Box Set

Contemporary Romance:
- ❖ Conflicting Hearts, by J.D. Burrows - Contemporary Romance/Women's Fiction (Finalist - Fiction/Social Issues – Readers' Favorite Book Award Contest 2017)

Sign up for my newsletter and blog by visiting my official website. Vicki Hopkins, Author - http://vickihopkins.com

The best way to thank an author, is to write a review.

Made in the USA
Lexington, KY
30 September 2019